The
Taco Tuesday
Murders

Barbara Krueger and Sean Todd

juniper
Publishing

Muchas Gracias

EL Chana

The Taco Tuesday Murders
Copyright © 2021 by Juniper Publishing

Sylvia • Antonio • Rosa • El Chano

The Celebrity Table

Don Diego • Manuel • Gladys • Juan • Clare

THE
TACO TUESDAY
MURDERS

Chapter One

The Mariachi

If you are not watching, you may miss it. A recently paved road, just beyond the curve, will take you to the clump of eucalyptus trees where the best Mexican Restaurant in town can be found. Jose, the owner, could only pave half of the parking lot that was now filled with cars. Even the graveled area, pitted with potholes and ruts, was overflowing. There was no more room to park. It was Taco Tuesday.

Clare's BMW bounced over the ruts and on to the grassy area under the Rhododendrons'. This wasn't really a parking space, but it was the only space left. The shoe that stepped out onto the grass was silver with a jeweled clasp. The leg was shapely, tanned and free from stockings. The dress was midnight blue with a full skirt just at the knee, perfect for dancing to the Mariachi that would serenade the patrons, just an hour from now.

She rustled her skirt, brushed back her auburn hair with her hand, applied some fresh lipstick, then headed towards the door as the lights overhead danced like stars across her dress. When Clare entered the restaurant, all heads turned. She took the three steps down into the dining room, with the grace of a trained professional. She was a dancer, and was scheduled to perform with the Mariachi's.

The large table to her left was nearly full, and a tall mustached senior quickly pulled out the chair to his right. All the men stood as she slid into her seat. Pleasantries were exchanged, but then the mood quickly darkened.

"What makes you think you can just slide in here as thought nothing had happened. You know what you did, Clare." Others tried to quiet Sylvia, but she stood and raised her voice even more, now, commanding the attention of the whole room.

"Alberto is dead because of you. I saw it!" she screamed. "His brains all over the floor, the gun still warm in his hand. You did this, Clare; you're a monster. You devour men and then you spit them out and kill them like a black widow." By now, several had to hold Sylvia back as she started lurching toward Clare.

Clare stood and shook her fist. "You lie, you viper among women. You know poor Alberto shot himself because you hounded him. He lost his business because you introduced him to those scoundrels. He said he played cards with them when he came back in town from a day on the desert. One day he brought back a black nugget that he said was worth about $1,200. He lost it, Clare, in one of those crooked games. What did they do, give you a share of the profits?"

Sylvia screamed, broke from her captives and grabbed Clare around the neck, shaking her like a rag doll. Clare reached for her eyes and managed to jab one long, blood-red fingernail into her eyelid. Sylvia screamed again, this time releasing her hold as the others clasped her around the waist and pulled her from the room. Clare sat down, washed her finger in the water glass, smiled as casually as she could, then sipped the glass of Chardonnay that magically appeared before her. "How can I perform," she questioned, her voice shaking slightly. "I am an artist and should not be exposed to such violence. Please Juan, help me to the dressing room where I can quiet myself and sip my Chardonnay in peace."

Juan obliged, placed his arm gently around her waist, and guided her from the room. A half sneer was barely discernable beneath his black mustache. The rest of the table sighed in relief.

Glasses clinked again, and the crunch of the taco shell informed everyone that the crisis was over.

By now the restaurant sounds were on the rise. There was a birthday party at the round table. Two men with guitars were serenading a young couple, as she shrieked with delight as a ring was placed on her finger. Several people stood at the front door, disappointed that there was no seating left. Everything had settled into a normal routine.

Then, they all slid their chairs back in order to see the entrance of the Mariachi's. The lights dimmed slightly, and a spot light announced their arrival. There was clapping and a few whistles as one of the largest bands of this type paraded into the room. There were ten handsome players, complete with sombrero, serapes, guitars of every size, two violins, and even two clarinets. The very air trembled, and everyone swayed and clapped to the music.

There was silence, and the Mariachi's formed a line from the small curtained stage. Nobody breathed. Then the blare of the trumpets and strum of guitars announced her arrival, and Clair, in shimmering red trimmed in gold, shot out from the curtain like a rocket. Her heels clicked, the castanets echoed the rhythm, as she swirled and twirled, and clicked some more. The audience was her captive and by the time she finished her dance they were all on their feet applauding.

The waiters filled the room taking drink orders as the mariachi's strolled around the tables. Clare would not perform for another hour, and usually she would join her friends for drinks and conversation. A half hour passed by; still no Clare. By now there was only one empty chair signifying her absence. The table started to buzz and their heads turned searching. Juan was still sitting next to her chair Gloria sat on his left and on her other side was her father, Manuel. Across, sat El Chano and his brother, Antonio, and sister Rosa, then, of course, the empty chair vacated by Sylvia.

Suddenly the loudest, most blood curdling scream shattered the air. Drinks dropped, chairs crashed, and patrons didn't know whether to run to the exit or hide under the table. Don Diego, the manager, did his best to calm the crowd and keep them in the restaurant until the police arrived. The person who let out that scream could not possibly have survived. But, survived what?

Chapter Two

Too Much Blood

After he put his waiters in charge of the now disoriented crowd, Don Diego followed what he thought was the direction of the scream. Previously, he had been standing by the curtain listening to the closing song of the Mariachi's before Clare's anticipated appearance. He climbed the small stage and through the curtains in the back, where there was a hallway to the kitchen and lavatory. He stood pondering, and saw Mimi peering around the door of the kitchen, eyes large and questioning.

"Did you hear it?" asked Don Diego

Mimi nodded, as though afraid to speak. Her eyes darted to her left, down the hall.

"The washrooms?" he asked? "

She shrugged, still afraid to speak.

Don Diego walked the 8 yards to the first door on the left, the opposite side of the dining -room. He felt sure the scream was female, so he slowly opened the ladies-room door. He was in the powder room, decorated with ornate mirrors and gilded chairs. On the other side of the room were velvet lounge chairs, and one chase for patrons who had more than enough to drink.

"Nothing here," he whispered to himself. He felt something tighten in his chest, his mouth was dry.. He even felt beads of sweat on his forehead as he walked slowly into the lavatory. The stall doors were all closed.

First, he called out, "Is anyone in here? The maintenance crew is coming. Let me know if there is anyone here before I allow them in." Nothing! Silence!

He inched forward to the first stall and nudged it open. Empty! He breathed a sigh of relief. There we six stalls. He took a deep breath and approached the second. The door swung open. Empty again.

The third and the fourth proved just as benign. Then he started toward the fifth. He felt a stickiness beneath his shoes. One more step and his hand was on the door,

It wouldn't budge. It was locked. Then, as he bent to look under the door, he saw two silver shoes that were more than familiar; the claps were no longer sparkling with jewels; they were covered with a substance that dulled the shine.

The door only left a little over a foot clearance to the floor, and didn't allow a broader view into the stall. The doors had been there for years and were almost as tall as the low ceiling, so he couldn't look over the top.

"Clare! Clare! Are you alright?"

A figure suddenly appeared behind him. "Don Diego! Don't touch anything," said El Chano. "The police have been called, and I thought it would be better if you weren't in here alone. Don't want any incriminating evidence or suspicion. Come on. I don't think she can hear us. Look at the floor."

The red sticky mass had oozed from inside the stall to a drain just outside the door. Both El Chano and Jose stood with their mouth open. "Let's get the hell out of here," yelled El Chano.

Chapter Three

Lieutenant Romero Roberto Mendoza (Bob)

The waiters had settled down the guests, mainly by serving free margaritas. However, before they could ask for another, the sirens screamed, and flashing red lights lit up the dining room through the windows on either side of the door. The long arm of the law had arrived in full force.

The first man to walk through the door should have been wearing a trench coat, but this was California, and over an hour away from Hollywood over the Grapevine. The town was Bakersfield, a legend in the oil industry, produce, citrus, plus some left-over cowboys. The almost legend in charge, was Lieutenant Inspector Ramero Roberto Mendoza, (Bob, to all his friends), and was unpretentiously dressed in blue jeans and classic grey golf shirt.

At his side, dressed also in jeans, and carrying a note pad, was his assistant, Luis Torres. You could easily identify the scientists; some were in white coats while forensics mostly wore blue jeans. Of course, Doc Paul

Patero wore his usual white jacket over jeans, complete with stethoscope, which, more than likely would not be needed.

The manager, Don Diego ran forward. He recognized the Lieutenant from previous trips to the restaurant. "Ok, where is the body, or is it still alive. The way your waiter sounded, I thought the whole place was under siege, "barked Bob.

"We are not sure, sir. You will see what I mean. She is locked in the stall."

"Stall? What is a stall?"

"Sir the women's lavatory. Come, I don't think she is alive but we couldn't get at her. Actually, we were afraid of disturbing any evidence for your boys," he gestured, as they followed him through the curtains.

"Hey, Meatball," the inspector called to one of the white coats. "First find out if she is alive so we know whether we have to break down the door."

Meatball, the largest among the white coats, got down on his amble stomach and felt for a pulse on her ankles, trying not to disturb the now drying blood on her shoes and floor.

"Dead as a doornail, sir, and if you don't mind my saying, there's a hell of a lot of blood."

"Go for it team. Dust the door for prints and open her up." yelled Bob,

"What, Jamie? It's locked from the inside? Ok, you know the drill. Check the hinges, the casing, everything. Damn, why can't anything be simple?"

The door finally came off and the scene that greeted them was no better than they thought it would be. Gasps were heard all around. Her head flopped forward, and even without seeing the wound, they all knew her throat had been cut.

"Find the damn weapon," asked Bob, this time a little less forcefully, as he held his handkerchief over his mouth, "And, try to stay out of the blood. Blood...too damn much blood. She's not large enough to hold that much, even if she bled out."

"Yeah, bled out," stammered Luis.

Bob took it upon himself to check the adjoining stalls and asked Luis to call Don Diego back.

Bob approached Meatball, "You say there was only a 12-inch clearance from the floor to the door? How much from the top of the door to the ceiling?"

"These restrooms were put in before all the modern plumbing techniques. Doors back then were tall and narrow. That only left a foot clearance to the ceiling; not enough for a human to get over or under,"

"You said human" questioned Bob, what were you thinking? Some animal carrying a blade climbed over and slit her throat? This is no science fiction thriller, Meatball. Hell, there isn't even enough room for a chimp, "

"The door was securely locked, Bob, with no sign of it being tampered with, as were all the nuts and bolts around the metal frame that attached the wood door to the fitting. All was secure. Hell, even the side walls were pristine. The stalls were well maintained; even looks like fresh paint."

As Don Diego walked up Bob pulled him aside. "When there is a plumbing issue, Diego, how does the plumber get to the pipes/ "Follow me," motioned Diego, as he headed down the hall past the men's rooms, where the hall took a turn to the left. There, a few feet down, was another tall, thin door. Diego pulled out his ring of keys, and opened the door to a narrow passageway with plumbing on the left wall,

"So, we are directly behind the lavatories? Where is the one we want?" asked Bob, not knowing what he expected to find

Diego counted down from the end, "This is the one, Look how pristine everything is. We had the whole restaurant painted a month ago; just before the grand opening of our new entertainment center. We can now attract some big names."

"This makes it easy for the plumber," said Bob. Your paint job makes it easy to see that nothing was tampered with."

"What were you looking for?" asked Diego.

"Don't know. There had to be some way into that stall; Some way to get a blade into the stall, cut her throat, and leave undetected, Sherlock Holmes could have figure it out. Remember his thriller, 'The Speckled Band?'" There was a tiny hole near the ceiling where a rope was pushed down that reached the sleeping victim. Then the snake was released. A snake that was trained by a whistle. Clever! Damn.. No hole at all for anything, even a wire to open or close the stall door.

Diego shrugged. "Seems to me, that is much too complicated. The killer must have had a tool that could open the stall door. It would only take seconds to slit her throat, lock the door with the same tool, and escape into the night.'

"Good theory. However, since your elaborate paint job, the screws and bolts were painted over and there was no sign of the tiniest scratch, Nope, this killer was too clever by far. Now let's let forensics finish. I want to go out and get those testimonies on what they are describing as a 'death rendering scream.'"

Chapter Four

The Scream

    Don Diego escorted Bob over to the table closest to the stage the table always reserved for the star performer and her entourage, this time the victim herself. Bob glanced around the table and his eyes stopped at an old friend. He was about to greet El Chano, when a waitress carrying a tray of Margaritas approached and quickly began passing them around. She looked questioningly up at Bob. Bob blinked twice then shook his head. She nodded, then walked away, her hips rocking seductively to the background music. He blinked again as he watched her blond hair, so out of place among the other raven beauties, also bounce to her step.

    He took a deep breath and turned back to the table. Diego slipped up beside him and whispered, "That's Stella from New Jersey. Pretty nice gal. Introduce you if you would like."

    Bob was noticeably flustered, but tried to hide his interest. Diego was not deceived. "When you are finished here, I'll call her over. She is a pretty good witness. Told me all about the scream and even noticed what the time was."

Bob nodded, happy to get back to the task at hand. El Chano stood as Bob approached. "Buenos Dias, amigo; so sorry to be meeting you under these circumstances. I would like to introduce you to my family; this is my sister Rosa, Rosa, meet the famous detective, Lieutenant Carlos Roberto Mendoza, known to his friends as Bob. And this is my brother Antonio, who was unfortunate to have dated that blue eyed blond that just delivered our drinks"

Antonio rose and bowed to Bob, "Unfortunate is correct. That is one cold bimbo, all the way from New Jersey. Couldn't get to first base."

Detective Luis walked up, smiling. El Chano, you know Bob's reputation."

"Si. I have lived here in Bakersfield most of my life: known Bob, for as many years as I have been in the contracting business. I had to call him in ten years ago when someone broke into my supply yard, killing one of my guards.

Bob nodde, still showing some pink around the collar from his almost introduction to Stella. He cleared his throat and turned to Luis. "OK, what do you have so far? Who heard what, and when, and where were they when they heard it?"

Luis flipped open his pad. "I'll start at the head of the table, boss. I have even made a diagram, so we remember where everyone was sitting at the time, Don Diego, you were seated at the table at the time of the scream, or were you still at the curtain?"

"It is hard to remember, exactly, but I believe I just sat down; tired of waiting for Clare to appear for her performance. I had already been to the dressing room, but no luck, so I returned here to be ready, in case I had to make an announcement."

"What kind of an announcement" pressed Bob.

"How the hell do I know. I didn't know what had happened to her. Only that she wasn't here. I was going to give her 15 more minutes, then call out the Mariachis'".

"OK, tell us about the scream?"

"I believe I had just sat down and then it came; so damn loud, everyone jumped. Some wanted to run or hide under the table. We didn't know what had happened. Stella is the best witness because she looked at her watch. She told me it was exactly 8:40. Clare was scheduled to perform at 8:30."

"What did you do then?"

"All I could think of was the patrons. They were ready to scatter, so I grabbed the mike and told them everything was under control and free Margaritas would be arriving right away. Then I got the waiters together, gave them crowd control instructions, and told the bartender to mix up enough drinks for the whole room. "

"What then?"

"I thought the sound came from behind the curtains off the rear hallway, so I ran in that direction. I saw Mina from the kitchen peeking her head around the corner, her eyes huge with fear. She pointed me toward the lavatories."

Bob urged him on. "OK, I found the stall and saw her shoes on the other side, now all soiled with what I thought was blood. I was about to try to open the door to see if she was alive, but El Chano stopped me. We both decided nothing could be done because of the amount of blood, so we left. Didn't want to disturb any evidence."

"Commendable of you. Now, who's next? Is everyone sitting in the exact same seat they were earlier; when you heard the scream?"

Everyone nodded. "There is an empty seat next to you Don Diego. Who was sitting there and when did they leave?."

There was silence for a minute before El Chano stood. "Lieutenant, there was a slight scene earlier this evening between the occupant of that chair, Sylvia, and Clare. It even came to blows and Sylvia had to be removed from the restaurant. I believe one of the waiters took her home."

"All right, I'll get the story from Sylvia, then Luis can take your statements. Right now, I am more interested in finding the time of death. The body has not given us the information because of the abundance of blood."

"All right, El Chano, it looks like you and your family are next according to the chart Luis has made for me. Let's start with you and then go to your brother and sister."

"I, too, looked at my watch," said El Chano. "I knew it was time for Clare's performance and wondered if this was some kind of sound effect for her new dance. Kind of seemed that way"

"In what way?"

"Too loud. Scared everybody. And I had the same time as Stella, 8:40. "

Bob looked over at Antonio and Rose as they both nodded their head vigorously

There were four seats on the opposite side of the table and it was obvious that the empty one was for Clare. Bob turned to the occupant next to Clare's chair.

Jose stood up and cleared his throat. I am Jose Cortège, and I was Clair's manager here in California. For some reason she decided to have one in each state where she performed. But I agree. I didn't look at my watch, but we all heard the scream at the same time. We were all here."

Gloria held tightly to Manuel's arm, scared to blink. "Si," said Manuel. "It is as they say. We all heard the scream at the same time. Can I take Gloria home now?"

"Shortly," murmured Bob as he looked over his notes. "Seems to me as though we have established the time of the murder. If the other patrons agree, we shall put it down at 8:40. Any disagreement?" Everyone nodded, as Bob walked away to confer with the other detectives.

It happened again. Not just one scream, but about 20 of them at one time. Bob ran to the center of the room, just in time to see 3 of the most colorful snakes he had ever laid eyes on slither across the floor heading straight for the guest table. Rose jumped up as one slithered under the table. Her movement startled the snake and it attacked. She screamed again. El Chano flung the table cloth over the snake. He looked around and saw a champagne bottle on an adjacent table. He grabbed it. The snake could clearly be seen jumping haphazardly under the cloth.

Rose was now back in her chair, holding her leg, tears streaming down her face as she muttered, "Am I going to die, am I going to die?" El Chano brought down the champagne bottle on what he thought was the head-end of the snake. The bottle shattered; the snake jumped once, then wriggled no more. Across the room a large man with number 12 shoes simply stepped on another snake. Now there was only one.

The customers, following the lead of El Chano, grabbed their table clothes and looked a lot like a circle of matadors waving the red clothes, with a very frightened, orange and yellow, two and a half foot snake, in the center of the ring. The crowd cheered.

Number 12 shook his head, walked over to the ring, with the air of a celebrity matador, and raised his leg to extinguish the snake. The snake leaped and bit his ankle. Number 12 let out a yelp and hobbled back to his table. The crowd cheered again.

The circle of red clothes moved in closer and closer to the snake. It was anticlimactic. Bob simply walked over, drew his pistol and fired. The show was over.

However, if anyone had been observing from the sidelines, they might have noticed the faces of two in particular, that appeared detached and amused by the performance, especially one whose smirky smile could be discerned beneath his elaborate black mustache, if only for seconds.

Now everyone concentrated on the two guests who were bitten. Paramedics were called and another flashing red light lit the room. El Chano rushed to his sister's aid while the inspector bent over number 12's ankle.

"Pretty swollen, but that is to be expected. I recognized that viper. Seen it over by the canyon a time or two. Looks a lot more dangerous than it is; kind of a cousin to one in South America, whose poison is pretty fast acting, and the anti-dote not always available.

The manager, Don Diego, had already instructed the kitchen to hurry with hot compresses and was applying one on Rosa when the paramedics arrived. They took one glance at the, now disabled snake, and nodded. "Looks lethal, doesn't he, but the Gilla Snake is only interested in smaller prey like lizards and insects. Loves spiders, I understand." He applied an estrangement, followed by an antibiotic cream, wrapped a gauze around the wound, and signaled his team to leave. The same procedure was applied to number 12, followed by an extended hush. For all intents and purposes, the show was over, and for a moment they seemed to forget that someone really died there that night.

Rosa smiled up at El Chano, "I really am feeling better. None of us really knew, did we, that the snake was harmless. I mean harmless to kill; had a good set of fangs, though," she laughed.

El Chano smiled back. "I think we should leave Rosa, but I want to talk to the Lieutenant for a second." Bob looked as though he, too, had finished whatever investigating could be done for the night, and began ushering the patrons out the door. El Chano walked up and motioned Bob aside.

Look Bob, I am taking a personal interest in this case. No, I promise I won't get in the way, but this affects family."

Bob nodded. "I understand, El Chano, but I would rather we work together than separately. You see, you have an advantage over me. People may talk to you where they walk away from me or find the need to lie, just so they don't appear guilty. I have to check on the guys in back, see what the doc has to say, and will be over at Haley's for a beer, after. How about a pow-wow?

I will be there, amigo, as soon as I see Rosa home. Brother, Antonio, has had one too many Margaritas and is not up to the task."

Bob slapped El Chano on the back, "See you in a few."

Once again the Lieutenant swept through the curtain to the back hall where the team was still at work. The body was being loaded onto the gurney, no longer dripping with blood. However, he turned left rather than right and entered the kitchen.

He had interviewed Mina before and headed straight for her table where she was busy stuffing mini corn-hens.

"You are not open for dinner tonight, are you?" he asked "Oh no, senior, we are preparing for a wedding feast. The guests will arrive tomorrow from the church around

4:00. There is much preparation. We are so happy that Mario's is doing the wedding cake so we don't have that problem." She laughed, "Last month we baked a four-layer cake, and when we placed it on the flowered table the layers started to slide. We saved the cake but it took all the wooden skewers we had left-over from the kabobs. Oh, dear God."

Bob couldn't hold back the smile, but he did stifle the laugh that had started to bubble up. "Senora, there are just a few questions that have been puzzling me, and I feel you are the very person to help me. You see, you told me that you heard the scream that everyone else in the dining room heard, but that you felt that it was not as loud as everyone seemed to think, further away. In fact, you felt that the scream was in the dining room and not in the lavatory, next door. Is that right?"

"Si, I heard the scream, but it was more muffled than everyone was saying. Because of that I was not as fearful. I did not feel that I was in immediate danger. It seemed like the victim could have been next door in the lavatory; where else? In fact, Maria asked for a bathroom break just a half hour earlier, and to the best of my remembering, she said nothing to arouse our suspicions. So confusing."

"A half hour earlier, you say. Did she see anything at all?"

"Senor, if the door was closed and someone was in the stall, what should we think? That they had their throat slit?"

"Yes, I see what you mean. Is she still here for me to talk to?"

"Si, we have much preparation. Do you want me to bring her? You can talk in my office. More private."

Mina directed Bob to the office. By the time Maria came sheepishly through the door, Bob was already ensconced in the swivel chair. He quickly rose and pulled over a folding chair that he had already prepared.

"Nothing to be afraid of, Maria. I just thought of something else that you might be able to help me with. Your testimony earlier was great, but now I need to know what you heard and saw when you were in the ladies' lavatory. Mina said you were there about a half hour before the scream. What did you see? Describe the scene as best as you can."

Maria took a breath and straightened her skirt. She squinted her eyes then, as though she could see better what she saw then. "I looked down the line of stalls. I noticed a door closed down at the end so I took the first one closest to where I came in. I still was surprised at the quiet, and wondered if there was really anyone else in the lavatory. When I was finished, I walked out into the powder room to wash my hands. Still no sound. Nothing."

"Did you see any feet under the stall at the end"?

"No senior. I am sorry I didn't bother to look. I was anxious to get back to work. I was preparing the strawberries for the fruit salad."

Bob nodded his head. "That is very helpful, Maria. You are a good witness. If I need anything else I will come to you."

Maria rose. She smiled as she walked out the door, feeling something like a celebrity.

Lieutenant Carlos Roberto Mendoza tried to stretch off the rigors of the day. He smiled as he thought of a tall, frothy ale, maybe accompanied by Haley's famous corned beef on rye. Then there was El Chano waiting for him. He nodded. Definitely something to look forward to after the events of the day.

"Events, hell!" he swore under his breath. "More like scenes from The Fifth Dimension." He climbed in his dark silver SUV and headed for the parkway.

Meanwhile, back in the restaurant, the arm of the law, as well as the customers had left. However, the kitchen crew was busy at work preparing the wedding feast, as someone else was cleaning up around the stage. He swept up the debris from the snake exhibition and straightened the palms that flanked the stage. No one noticed the only other occupant at the celebrity table who appeared to be fast asleep. His head rested on the now crumpled table-cloths that partially hid his face. It was Juan, Clare's manager. He looked up just as the broom left the room, with a puzzled expression on his face.

"Hmmm, I wonder." Then he quickly grabbed his sweater and sprinted to the door.

Many of the waitresses were asked to stay in the kitchen where they could help with the feast. Stella, the blond waitress, of Bob's previous admiration, was just finishing the green beans. She looked over at Mina, got the nod, hung up her apron, and walked out into the cool of the evening. The moon was full and lit up the parking lot which helped her hand that had begun to shake as she clicked for the car door to open. She was parked on the gravel, some distance from the restaurant and nearly dropped the keys as she distinctly heard a crunch to her right. She struggled with the door. Another crunch. Now she was visibly shaken.

"Why won't the damn door open?" Another crunch, and as the door finally opened, a figure stepped into the moonlight.

"You should have had someone walk you to your car. Did you forget we have a murderer on the loose; someone with a blade sharp enough to cut your throat?"

"Thanks a lot Don Diego for calming my nerves. I didn't forget; that's just it. We are all scared to hell and back, but you are right; we should never be alone."

With that, Stella started the car, locked the door and belted. As she drove out of the parking-lot she noticed Don Diego standing there watching her. "Kind of comforting having someone looking after me." she smiled, "I hope he had more of a weapon than that old broom."

By the time Stella drove into a space near the front door of Haley's Bar and Grill, Bob was holding up his glass for a refill. He was ready to bite into his corned beef sandwich when he looked up and saw Stella walk in the front door. His mouth was open, poised for that first, long-awaited taste, looking much like a kid at the candy store.

Stella looked over, saw the Lieutenant, and waved. When he came to his senses, Bob waved back, and didn't realize his wave was taken for a "join us" gesture. Pleased not to be alone, Stella joined their booth and waited for Bob, still unable to put thoughts together, to move over and allow her to sit. El Chano just looked on, biting hard on his lip to keep it from smiling.

"Beer?" asked Bob, still unable to put a sentence together.

Stella shook her head. "No, thank you, a Chardonnay for me, with a glass of ice on the side.

"Boy, am I ready for this," she smiled at the waitress, as she pointed her finger at Bob's sandwich, "one of those too, please.

"El Chano, I know you from the restaurant; you usually sit at the celebrity table. I also know your brother, Antonio, who is definitely not the gentleman you are. Ha! I see by both your expressions that you have heard of my reputation. Si, as you both would say, I am very selective when it comes to men." She took two healthy gulps of her Chardonnay, leaned back in the booth and thoroughly enjoyed the silence. Both men were speechless.

Once Stella's sandwich arrived, the men felt they could resume their conversation and jumped right into the theatrics of the snake show.

"Quite a performance, mi amigo," smiled El Chano. I felt all along it was staged for a single purpose, one which simply escapes me. Do you agree?"

Bob wiped the foam from their lips. "Yes, there was no reason to release three snakes that created such chaos among the patrons as those did. Kind of like the shell game. Do I keep my eye on the pea or the three shells, or perhaps on what is being palmed by the performer? All along I felt I was being had; and very cleverly, at that. I have gone over and over the scene in my mind's eye, as they say, and it was so hard not to look at the snakes. I have the film from the camera that always surveys the dining room. Nothing; at least nothing, yet. I am going to have my men go over it with a fine- tooth comb. I know the killer had a good reason to pull such a stunt. Trust me. El Chano, we'll figure it out. If you have any bright ideas, let me know. We are in this together; I am going to need your inside help.

Bright eyed and feeling much better, Stella's eyes grew big. "Does that include me, too, I hope. I have always considered myself a pretty good sleuth. I can also do some undercover work. I work there, Chano doesn't. I see and hear a lot and could report back every few days. What about it chief?"

"First of all, I am not a chief, second of all," he paused, thinking of the idea of meeting with Stella every few days a better than good idea, he reluctantly said, "we'll give it a try. You will have to watch your step and please don't confide with anybody about our liaison."

"Oooo, that makes it sound more sleuth-like. OK boss, you are on, but for now this working girl has to get some sleep. We've got a wedding tomorrow, sure wish it was mine."

As she walked away, Bob's face was noticeably redder. El Chano rose and slapped his friend's back. Well, I definitely do not have a wedding tomorrow, but I do need my sleep. Buenos Naches.

Bob ordered another draft, and tried to relax. "Damn that woman. Now I can't think straight." He smiled, "Maybe that's not a bad thing."

Twenty minutes later, El Chano's Mercedes, S560 drove into the underground parking garage of his condo building. He clicked the lock button and was starting toward the elevator when he heard a scream. He stopped and listened thinking he had heard enough screams for a lifetime. However, it came from his right so he started to run. He felt in his pocket for his Beretta. He nodded and kept running, hoping she would scream again. She did!

Then he heard the scuffle behind the car ahead, and saw a woman's purse being raised and brought down swiftly. It was quiet. His gun was drawn as he rounded the car. The girl with the purse raised it again.

"A gun. Come on," she panted, 'you can't be serious."

"Thought you were in trouble. What the hell do you have in that purse that brought him down so fast?"

"Rocks! Good old-fashioned rocks from the road-side."

"I assume he was accosting you, right?"

"Damn right. He lives in this building and has been laying in wait for me for weeks. He figured he had a good night for his pursuits because I am home so late. Can you believe, he actually grabbed me and tried to force me into the back seat; the pervert."

El Chano walked over to the unconscious predator, took some hand-cuffs from his rear pocket, clicked them closed, then dialed.

"Hey, Bob. I just cuffed a guy in my garage. What should I do with him? OK, Bill Parker. Si, I will ask for him. Sweet dreams. Just thought you might like to hear my 'scream story' of the night. Ohhhh..." he turned to the brunette. "He hung up!"

After the sirens had gone with their package neatly wrapped, El Chano turned to the girl and bowed, introducing himself.

"Are you a policeman?" she asked.

"Nope, just a friend of the Lieutenant. Now, what is your name, if I may ask, as he assessed the neat 5'4" frame of this petite fighter that made his 5' 10" look pretty good.

"Sydney," she replied, "Sydney Young. And no, I am not a professional fighter or wrestler. You can put your arm down and stop intimidating me with your biceps, which tells me that you also work out. I work out over at Young's Gym down the street. It belongs to my dad and he makes sure I have a peaceful workout. Guys can be pretty obnoxious at times," she smiled, as she reached over and squeezed his right upper-arm.

"I work out there every Sunday night and sometimes on Wednesday, if I have the time. I don't remember seeing you."

"I'm there most mornings before work," she explained. "I work over at the Bone Yard; you know, that hang-out for archeologists just in from the desert or mountains with their burlap bags full of bones. Then we try to reconstruct the dinosaur."

"You're kidding, not dinosaurs."

"Jest, if you must, but we started on Jackson almost six months ago now when the first collection came in that we finally determined came from a prehistoric. Pretty big stuff, when you think about it. I'll have to show you around sometime. But now, this working girl is for bed unless you want a quick night-cap to close a perfectly unusual evening. Come on up if you please, I have a nice bottle of Bailey's that needs opening."

El Chano didn't have to think but merely nodded and followed Sydney into the elevator. She was still in her work clothes, and the lab slacks she wore accentuated the line of her derriere that told more than she realized.

Once in her condo, El Chano let out a whistle. There was one full wall with silver framed glass bookcases, all filled with bones of every shape and size.

"Can I touch?" he asked politely.

She went to the table under the window that was rarely used for dining, but was now covered with an assortment of acquisitions.

"You can play with these" she smiled, while I get the drinks.

El Chano began to brush the sand away from what looked like someone's femur, when she handed him his Baileys on the rocks. She walked to the far side of the room where a giant white sectional faced the largest TV he had ever seen in captivity.

"This is nice," he said. "Not bad for somebody who digs stuff up that has been buried for thousands of years. You must like it?"

"It was kind of boring before the prehistoric. I used to work in Jerusalem. There are more digs there than you can imagine. Of course, the monks often have the prize locations, like the one on the Mt. of Olives," she yawned.

"Oh, oh," he said, as he stood. "That is my cue to vamoose. We both need our sleep." He thought for a minute as he set down his glass, not wanting to depart without sealing another get-together. How about dinner some time next week. You have to eat sometime."

"Usually around 7:00 on Wednesday," she laughed.

"All right," he smiled. "If that's when they feed you, and it's after your work-out, we had better eat heartily. How about Mama Rizzo's?"

"Wednesday at Rizzo's," she said, as they reached the door and gave his arm one more squeeze. You can call for me here."

By the time El Chano reached the elevators, the corners of his mouth broadened to a full smile, and by the time he was inside, heading for two floors above, a very loud yahoooo could be heard. That is, if anyone was around to hear it.

Chapter 5

When is a Clue Not a Clue?

Lieutenant Bob was at his desk. It was 8:05 and the steam was still coming off his coffee; the jelly donut was still untouched. The reports from forensics were coming in, but Doc's report was still absent.

"I could have written it myself," he mumbled. "Her throat was slit; that is unless she was poisoned first, then shot, and was cut, just to be sure."

He made up his mind; picked up his coffee cup, but decided to leave the donut behind. Last time he brought food to the Doc's horror chamber with corpses lined up like a smorgasbord, he lost both his breakfast and lunch.

Doc was holding a tube of blood up to the light. He turned as Bob walked in. "Her blood tests 'A' positive, but something is different. What did this bimbo eat and drink? Could she be the first vampire we've had down here? Unnatural amount of blood, that's what I say."

"Come on Doc. You're pulling my leg, right?"

"Only the vampire part. And that's only because I haven't personally had one on my table. This is the first one that could come close. However, it is my theory that if she was a vampire her type would be 'O,' because of the variety of victims."

"Maybe she was selective, Doc. Just like I know you like raised chocolate donuts, and I like jelly filled. See, selective."

Doc threw a rag, already soiled with blood. "Hell, Bob, this just isn't a clue we can work with. I'll have to send samples to the lab downtown. God knows we've got enough blood for a hundred tests. We'll get the answers."

Bob didn't have the stomach to throw the rag back, but instead thought of the donut waiting for him upstairs.

He took the elevator up and as he stepped out he could already see that a theft had taken place. His voice vibrated around the large room. "Luis!"

Sprinting from the men's room, Luis, second in command, stood apprehensively at Bob's desk. "What's up, boss."

Bob spastically pointed his finger at his desk.

"Which report, boss?" he asked, still not understanding why Bob would be so upset by early forensic reports. "I didn't see anything we can use yet. They pegged the time of death at around 8:40 according to that Stella person."

"She is not a Stella Person, her name is Stella Walker, and she was the only one that bothered to check the time. The donut, where's my jelly donut?"

Luis's face turned red. He stammered, "I ate it boss. You know how sometimes you bring one for me? Well, I thought this was one of those times. You weren't here, and your coffee was gone."

"Great detective you are. Did it ever occur to you that I might be working on something, say in the morgue with Doc.? You know I don't bring food down there."

That's why you are the Lieutenant, boss. I'll have six jelly donuts here tomorrow morning."

"Who's going to eat all six?"

"Just a figure of speech; I'll have two, and I will guard them with my life."

Bob almost smiled, but didn't. After all, nobody messes with your jelly donut. "Now we have to get over to the restaurant. Two things in his report need checking on. Let's go."

The wedding dinner/reception wasn't until 4:00, so Bob figured he had plenty of time to poke around.

"Poke around?" yelled Don Diego, "we have over a hundred people showing up here at 4:00 and they expect to be entertained and fed. The last thing they want to see is a couple of policemen interrupting the festivities."

"Now hold on, Don Diego. There are just two minor items in the report that we need to check. Shouldn't take but an hour. You know I can be discrete."

"Discrete, hell; when were you ever discrete? You'll probably knock over the floral display, the punch bowl, and confiscate the cake, thinking the murder weapon was baked inside."

Don Diego threw up his hands and walked away, knowing that his words fell on deaf ears, or rather "stubborn ears," he smirked to himself.

The Lieutenant led Luis to the back hall and around to the plumbing door. Once inside he instructed him. "There has to have been some way to reach the lavatory on the other side of this wall where the victim was slain. The fresh paint makes it difficult, but that was painted a month ago. Now, if there was a hole of some kind it still had to be painted over. Feel for anything out of the ordinary, a bump, indicating spackling, or paint that is a little different color than the rest. I know, I know, it's a long shot, but it's the only shot we have right now."

"Sir?" questioned Luis, "you are not trying to say that the killer could get a blade through some kind of hole?" As soon as he said it he wished he hadn't. The look that Bob gave him said volumes, so he got to work carefully running his hand over the wall.

Each one caressed the wall as gently and inquiringly as he could. Bob stopped. He took his pencil and circled the area. Then he started to knock on the wall, looking for a sound change. He smiled, then picked up his cell phone and dialed.

"George, did you get everything I asked for? Yes, that's it; now bring it around to the plumbing room. Try not to let Don Diego see you. He's going to kill me, but it can't be helped. Hurry, let's get this over with. When George arrived, he pulled out his drill, prepared to cut a two-inch diameter opening, and turned it on. It didn't take long to cut through the plaster-board, then they all worked feverously to clean up.

"Thank God for new products," he said, as he placed a mesh on the opening, patched, waited a second or two and painted. George ran around to the stalls and did the same. Luck was with them. No Don Diego.

George was gone as fast as he arrived, and Luis just shook his head. "I don't get it yet, boss. I know you figure there is a hole inside the one that George just cut out, but I still don't see the point."

"You will, just hold on. Every locked room mystery has an explanation, and most of the time it is the simplest one. You see, the killer had to have an exit plan. The lavatory door had to be locked to draw us away from the knowledge that the killer didn't need a device to unlock it to get in."

"But why didn't he need a way to open the door? Doesn't make sense. How did he get in?"

Bob shook his head. "He didn't need a prearranged way to get in, Luis, because it is my theory that she wasn't killed in the stall at all."

'But the scream, not to mention the volumes of blood running down the drain," Luis complained.

"Think about it, Luis. What do all these things, put together, remind you of?"

They took one last look around at their handy-work and saw no trace of their shenanigans. Once in the car, heading back to the park-way, Luis couldn't hold it in any longer. "Come on, boss. What is it supposed to remind me of?"

"The Theatre, my good man, the theatre."

Chapter 6

The Illusion

"It's the old shell game, again. There was a point during the snake scene, that's exactly what it was, a scene, created for a very specific purpose. My guess, without really knowing, is that there was something that needed to be retrieved before my men finished their investigation. I believe that something was removed, and it's going to take some great reconstruction on our part, to figure out how and what it was"

"I can see where you are going with this, Bob, and it is a doozie. You have to be right, because it's the only scenario that makes any sense. Wow, we are dealing with one clever dude. Who's that clever? Wait a minute, there's just one man I can think of. Noooo, not really," said Luis, "could it be?"

Bob raised his eyebrows and cocked his head, "We'll see Luis, we'll see. I just hope he is content with one murder, that's all. I would hate to see what he would do with another one."

El Chano was the only one with foresight. He at least secured a dinner date for the following Wednesday with Sydney. When he rang the doorbell. he brushed off any imaginary debris from his jacket and tried to hide the flowers behind him, questioning his impulsiveness.

She opened the door and immediately tried to peek around his shoulder. Chano, they're beautiful. "Please, may I," she said, and reached for the bouquet.

He was also mouthing the word beautiful, but it didn't come out. It just bounced around as he took in the pale pink dress that fit her like a glove and bounced around her knees as she motioned him in, then ran to the kitchen to place the flowers in a vase. Before he knew it her arm was laced in his and she hurried him out the door saying, "come on, I'm starved."

El Chano took no chances. He called ahead to secure a table; not just any table, but one far enough from the fountain where one could talk and not be sprayed.

Sydney noticed the ambiance immediately, and smiled. "This is beautiful, Chano, look at the flowers around the fountain. How romantic."

As soon as they were seated, a young lady approached them with a basket of white and pink roses. Tears came to Sydney's eyes. A hand came to cover her mouth. She looked over at Chano. Not a word needed to be spoken as Chano reached over and chose six roses, all pink. A vase was quickly supplied, and the flowers placed near to Sydney for her full enjoyment.

She beamed. "They are so beautiful, Chano, my very favorite. Thank you"

"You do get to take those home, you know. I do hope six is enough; I thought a dozen would block my view of something even more beautiful."

By now Sydney's face was the same color as her dress, but she was noticeably pleased with the compliment. She picked up the menu just as the champagne was poured. "My cup runnith over," she smiled.

Chano suggested the veal, and the Marcella surpassed itself. "No question," he thought to himself, "this is the most perfect evening I have ever experienced." He was about to invite Sydney to his condo for a couple of French pastries to be washed delicately down by a rare cognac when his cell phone rang.

Reluctantly, he picked it up and saw it was Bob. "Where the hell are you?" he asked. "Doesn't matter, were ever you are get home immediately. There is a fire in your condo, on the 5th floor."

Chano tried not to look too alarmed. "Are you there?"

"Where else would I be except maybe on a date having a good time like maybe, you are. Get over here, pronto; they say they suspect arson."

Sydney was watching the worried expression on Chano's face. "OK, what is it. Homicide?"

"No, at least, I don't know. Right now, it is arson."

They piled into the Mercedes. El Chano didn't tell Sidney where they were going. He knew her suspicions would accelerate after the next turn.

"Chano, look! The cars are backed up all the way to 9th. Chano! The ladder truck is there and it's at our condo! Chano, why didn't you tell me. Oh, I see. How close is it to our condos?"

"As far as I know, Bob said it was isolated on the 5th floor. That's mine, and two above is yours. Look, there's Bob, waving us through."

Bob waved them behind his car and they jumped out. Sydney forget her roses and kept staring at the building, a half block away, smoke coming out the windows on the 5th floor. El Chano started counting from the left. "Bob! You didn't tell me it was my condo. How bad is it?"

"It started in the elevator shaft just one down from your place. They are thinking they can save most of yours from the flames, but the smoke damage will be extensive. Sorry, my amigo. You must have ruffled a few feathers to have brought this much hate. That is, if you were the intended."

"How are the rest of the floors?" asked Sydney. "I am two below Chano's"

"You should be OK. Look at the water they are streaming on that place. Say, Chano, I just discovered that it was your construction company that recently remodeled and painted the restaurant we are investigating. How about we all go down the street and talk about it. Nothing we can do here for quite a while. Hell, what a mess."

They all piled in the Mercedes and headed for Rancho Grande, one of the few Mexican restaurants they knew would be open late. Once all the greetings and sympathies were over they piled into an ample booth in the back. When the tray of drafts arrived, even Sydney eagerly picked up hers. She drank until her upper lip was foamed.

"No toasts tonight," she mumbled. Seems like what we need are some solutions to a very complicated puzzle. That is, if there is a connection between the fire and your murder case, Lieutenant."

Bob tried to smile, but couldn't. "Pretty astute of you Sydney. How did you put that together?"

"My dad taught me that there are very few coincidences in life, if any at all, and looking at your expression tells me that you just dropped the connecting bomb."

"Bob, Sydney is smarter than your average, and likes to dig up stuff. She is an archeologist. And, yes, I remember doing quite a bit of work for the restaurant. That is a month ago, now. We did a lot of construction work on the stage and the kitchen, and then painted the whole place inside and out. But, what connection could that be to the murder?"

Bob was staring at Sydney, "We should ask your bright archeologist about that. What do you say, Sydney?"

She smiled back at Bob. "I am always up for the challenge, but I know so little about the case. However," she put up her hand to silence her critics, "that had to be something that you and your crew saw or knew about that would incriminate someone. Who is the owner, the one who ordered the job?"

"That would be a Senior Sanchez, but he sold some of his stock, I understand, and the shareholders now own the restaurant, theoretically, of course."

"Ah," exclaimed Sydney, "but who is the largest share-holder?"

"That remains to be seen," said Bob. "We are looking into it now. My next question is, what could have been done to the place that would draw any connection at all to the need to kill that poor gal."

"Could just be a smoke screen," ventured Sydney. "Somebody just didn't like her, that's for sure, but it takes more than that to take a blade to some ones throat; at least I hope it does."

El Chano finally broke in. "Seems like this whole murder was elaborately planned, down to all the diversionary tactics, snakes included. OK, Bob, you started to explain a theory of yours, something to do with the shell game?"

"Not the shell game, in particular," he said, "just the art of illusion. If, as we believe, the snakes were thrown in the mix as a diversionary ploy, then that means the illusionist, (murderer), wanted everyone looking at the shells and not what might be palmed in his hand."

Let me tell you what I am thinking. The word I threw at Luis earlier was "Theater." I believe everything was staged, all for a specific reason, but also for an overall effect. Damn, it worked! Seems like we fell for each and every false clue as it was thrown in our face. I haven't figured out all of them. It is obvious that the snakes were used to cover up something the murderer had to do. While we were all watching the shells, (the snakes), the killer palmed something. Just don't know what that something was."

El Chano furrowed his brow, "Seems to me that the construction of the stage must have had something to do with it. Probably the paint job, too. But that would directly point to the owner or one of the stockholders as the killer.

51

No, too simple, and this killer is anything but simple. He might even be doing it again. He knew we would be looking into the remodeling as part of the plot. Old shell game again? I give up Bob."

"No, we are not totally wrong. Can't figure the snakes, but the paint job was part of covering up the locked room lavatory. We found the hole in the wall. Either a wire or string was passed through to lock the door after the killer was done with his murder display. I say it was fishing line. Experimented with it, and the plastic line would leave no marks and could easily pull the bolt shut then release it's hold and be pulled back through the hole. The hole was so small we could barely see it, and was undoubtedly spackled with one tiny swipe after the fact. All you would need would be one finger of spackle and a tiny dab of paint. The same with the plumbing off the hall."

"Wait a minute" said Sydney, "that explains how he exited and locked the stall behind him, but how did he get in? She was in the stall and would put up a fight if someone tried to break in while she was doing her business."

"Ah," said El Chano. "That's the catch, isn't it Bob? They didn't have to break in. They just placed her on the throne, left, and pulled the string from behind the wall. Easy."

Sydney gulped, "Are you both trying to say that she was already dead when they placed her in the lavatory? But that is sick. Who would do a thing like that?"

"If we knew that the case would be over. But there is one more problem with the scene," explained Bob. "Doc was having a lot of problems with the amount of blood, type, 'A,' to be exact. So much blood, that at one time Doc even alluded to the possibility that she was a vampire. He laughed and said she would have to be type 'O," instead of 'A.'"

"You're right," said El Chano, "When I first came on the scene to warn the manager, Don Diego, there was a lot of blood coming from the inside of the stall and running to the drain, outside. We could see her shoes caked in blood. She had to be dead, so I pulled him away to wait for the authorities. No unwanted clues, you know. Yes, I pushed the door with my elbow. It was locked."

"What a gross scene," said Sidney. "Could it have been pigs blood they sprinkled around.? They say pigs have a lot of blood."

Bob and El Chano stared at Sidney. "Sprinkled around," said Bob. "Brilliant Sydney, but no, it was human, type 'A.'"

"Yes," mused El Chano. "However Sydney, other blood could have been released. A whole bag full of it, actually. But where could they get her blood type, or even know what type it was?" he asked.

"Remember" said Bob, "this whole performance was skillfully planned,"

"The blood bank," yelled Sydney, proud of her announcement,

Bob dialed his phone and was quickly connected to the blood bank downtown. After asking a few questions, he smiled at Sidney. "They just discovered it. They don't inventory every day, but it just so happens that they came up with two liters of type 'A' missing this morning. They had a call from an accident on the freeway. Coincidence, Miss Sidney?"

She shook her head

Chapter 7

Another Surprise

Bob left both El Chano and Sydney at the Harvest Inn, just a few blocks from the condo. Neither one wanted to face the remnant of the fire. Yes, the trucks were gone and the scene was almost back to normal, except for the amount of water on the streets and the blackened bricks around the 5th floor. Bob enjoyed the walk back to his car. His head was spinning.

"I don't get it yet," he said to himself, "but I am beginning to separate fact from fiction. Just beginning. His thoughts went to El Chano and Sydney, and he thought they made a good couple. Then he thought of Stella, and smiled. Yes, he did call her, and yes, she did say she would meet him for dinner at Domingo's tomorrow night. He just hoped he would be able to make it. This case was starting to get him down. "Down, down the drain. Too much blood, now stolen from the blood bank. But why? Oh, hell, I need some rest." He went home.

El Chano breakfasted at the hotel café with Sydney. Hardly breakfast, he thought with just coffee and croissants sitting in front of each of them, now looking a little worse for wear; them, not the croissants. No, it was not a time for romance, thought El Chano. Nothing romantic about a fire, especially one that could have destroyed his belongings.

"Hmmm," he thought to himself. "What do I have that I can't live without?" Sydney looked up and saw his pensive expression.

"Thinking about the fire?" she asked. "I am, and I don't think I have lost anything. However, by your expression, you have some valuables, don't you?"

"Mostly just the art. Furniture can be replaced. Clothing can be replaced, but the paintings from Madrid, and the sculpture from Vatican City, not so much."

"But, Chano, even paintings can be restored. Bob said the flames didn't get inside, just smoke. I know your treasures will be fine. Anyway, it is always fun to get a new wardrobe."

El Chano made a face, but secretly agreed with her. "Yes, a new wardrobe, and maybe even one that will travel to the Caribbean. I have to do something while the condo is being restored," he thought. "Hmmm, wonder if Sydney would go?" he mused as she looked at him quizzically.

"Not sure I can read that expression," she said. "not sure I want to."

They both laughed, actually ate their croissants, and finally were ready to check the fire damage. Well, half-heartedly, at least.

It was a fine morning for a walk. They slowed down the last block as they saw the building down the street. They didn't realize, but their hands met and they finished their walk holding on to the newfound security in each other.

They walked up to the front door and Justin, the doorman, was surprisingly on duty.

"No police?" asked El Chano.

"They all left around dawn, except for the team sifting through the rubble in the elevator shaft. They are using the service elevator on the other side of the building. You, Miss Sydney, can go up, but El Chano, you will have to be cleared by the inspector.

"Any idea how much damage was done, Justin?"

"Only one condo sems to have been scorched. That is the one directly next to the elevator. Seems like they started the fire in the elevator on the first floor, then sent it up to the 5th. Pretty clever."

"A sick kind of clever," said Sydney. "Come on Chano, let's walk around to the service elevator. I have an idea your good friend, the Lieutenant, is still on the premises. Just a hunch from what you have told me."

"Well, Sydney wins again," thought El Chano as he saw Bob standing outside the service entrance talking to the fire chief.

Sydney stopped before she entered and turned to Chano, "Say, if you want food or drink or anything, just pop up."

Bob heard her remark, and his eyebrows went up as El Chano bent over to give her a delicate peck on the cheek. "Be up later."

Once she was gone Bob shook his head. "I suppose you want to take a look at your place. I saw it, and everything is intact. No flames. The condo two down was gutted, and the one next to you got soaked. Yours is dry, but smoke damaged. Come on, I'll take you up. I hope you want a new wardrobe. Never liked that pink shirt of yours, anyway"

El Chano laughed as he followed Bob up the service elevator to the 5th floor. Chano reached for his handkerchief and held it over his mouth. "Putrid, isn't it? It will take some work to get the building back to its former glory."

Bob pulled out a key that fit the new temporary lock that the fire department put on because they had to break in,

"Nobody wanted any theft, Chano; you've got some expensive art in here. Seems to me everything is restorable except for the soft goods, like furniture and clothing."

"I consider myself lucky. This is all doable. I'm even remembering some grey slacks I saw at The Men's Depot. Don't worry Bob, I'll make lemonade." He walked around the condo and ran his finger across one of the paintings. "Not too bad. Easy clean. I consider myself lucky."

"Well, maybe not as lucky as you would like to be. Come on across the street, and let me buy you a cup of coffee and Danish. I have news for you. You will not be pleased"

Once inside the booth, El Chano leaned forward. "OK, how bad is it? Is brother Antonio and Rosa all right?"

"I was told," said Bob, "that your brother Antonio did a little boasting the night of the murder about his conquests. He said that if he wanted a girl, he usually got her. I think after missing the boat with Stella, he was doing a little ego building. Clare seemed to be his next conquest. He even went on to say that if he didn't get her, nobody else would."

"Whew," whistled El Chano. "That hot-headed brother of mine. He does this all the time, thinking he is this centuries' Romeo. Damn fool,"

"Well, evidence started piling up. He did a lot of boasting around town, then the threats started. Seemed that he had to save face. We found a couple of toilet items in

Clare's apartment that he said weren't his, but we proved they were. El Chano, we had to arrest him. He is in County for the time being."

"Damn!"

"Want a Danish?"

"No thanks. But I do want to help. You said you needed an insider. Do you mind if I get the scoop from my oversexed brother, and maybe Rosa, too, if she will tell me anything?"

"I was hoping you would say that. Let me finish my Danish and we can head downtown. I don't know where my next meal is coming from. I was hoping to spend it with Stella tonight. One can always hope."

After leaving the restaurant with Bob, El Chano got permission to return alone to his condo. He walked around his former sanctuary in a daze. He felt like he had lost his best friend. "No, not lost," he said to himself, "just suddenly unfamiliar. I can't even change my socks. Clothes, maybe that should be the first thing on my agenda—clothes. Ok, then maybe a place to live for the month it will probably take to make this home again."

He shook his head. "Si, I have a plan. But first, I must visit Antonio, who needs a swift kick; maybe three. Mon Due, who needs a brother like this?"

Bob saw El Chano leave the building and felt for his old friend. "Funny how families can produce such opposites. Now I have to see the new evidence that the Chief has turned up."

The manager of the building had turned over an alcove in his first floor office to Bob, so he could more easily display what might or might not be important evidence; that is after the arson squad finally started sharing. Captain Downing pointed to two items on the table.

"We believe the fire was detonated remotely by a cell phone simply calling a specific number that sparked the first charge. There were three; all charges connected by this type of wire here." He held up a black wire, innocent looking by itself, "but in this case," explained Downing, "just about anything could be transmitted."

"Transmitted, huh?" asked Bob. "I've seen this wire before. It looks suspiciously like one we picked up at the murder scene in the Mexican restaurant. Damn, I had a feeling all along that there was a connect, but didn't have enough dots. Say, Chief, is there any way I can get a piece of this wire to match to a piece we found at our murder scene? And what is this crumpled piece of plastic over here?"

"That, my friend, is a burned and melted-down cell phone. Pretty clever, huh? After he laid the explosives, the phone became the detonator. The elevator was sent to the 5th floor. Our arsonist got himself a safe distance away, probably where he had an alibi. When he was ready, he just dialed the number, and poof; the phone in the elevator received the call. Boom! Fire! The condo next to the shaft was the only one that was badly burned."

The Chief reached over, took out the wire clippers and gave him a generous three inches of the wire. He picked up a tag, now duly labeled and signed. Bob smiled his thanks, waved, and headed downtown. Now his smile broadened. Maybe he could make that dinner tonight, after all.

Meanwhile El Chano sat across from Antonio in the interrogation room at the county jail. Two guards were posted outside. Chano was staring at his brother, but could barely see his eyes. Antonio looked at the floor, the table, even the faded picture of a lone cactus on the desert, intended to illustrate the criminal's state of isolated misery.

"Did you do it, Antonio? Did you kill that woman?

"Hell, no. Why should I kill her? She was putty in my hands."

"Damn, Antonio, cut the crap. You're talking to your brother, now. Why did you lie to the Lieutenant? Why did you say the toiletries were not yours? They were not incriminating in themselves."

How should I know that?" squeaked Antonio. I thought he was setting a trap."

El Chano knew that his brother would lie if he felt trapped. "Hell, he didn't do it," he said to himself. "Too dumb, by far. This killer was too smart, by far. Bob and I might know who it is, but it's going to be a cold day down below, before we can prove it."

He slapped Antonio on the back, knocked on the door, and breathed a sigh as the prison doors closed behind him. He looked at his watch and saw it was only 1:30, with plenty of time for clothes, and hotel for the night. "Maybe I should take a cruise for a month and forget the whole damn thing. No, I can't. Antonio is my brother, and no matter what, family comes first. I owe it to mom."

It was two hours later that an exhausted El Chano loaded his car with more boxes that one would think possible in such a short period of time.

'Multiples," said El Chano. "That's the secret. Five pairs of slacks, two sport coats. Two sweaters, seven knit shirts, and five semi-dress shirts, socks, two pairs of shoes, and heaps of underwear. Done; and even a suitcase, should I decide to leave town."

His cell phone rang.

"Sydney. Good timing. I just finished shopping, have all new duds, and am about to check into the Empire for a few nights. Dinner? No, no plans, and, yes, I can be at your place by 6:00. Need time to shower and change. Thanks, Sydney. See you in a few."

So, here we are. Day three at the murder scene is coming to a close, and not too soon for some. Back at the restaurant, Stella was finishing her shift when Don Diego walked over.

"Is there any chance you can stay on for another hour? Rita called in sick and we are about to get busy."

"Sorry Boss, I've got a heavy date tonight with our Lieutenant. Wouldn't miss this for the world."

Stella watched him walk away, feeling a tad sorry for him, but not enough to change her plans. He bent to tie his shoe. picked up a cocktail napkin, then walked away. She shook her head, thinking that the murder was too much for the poor man. "Even looks like he is losing weight. Wonder if he eats the food here?" she laughed, as she grabbed her sweater and walked out into the Bakersfield night.

Chapter 8

Time Out for Romance

El Chano took his time preparing for his dinner engagement, wondering all the time if she really knew how to cook. He laid out the new light grey slacks, neatly pressed by housekeeping, and stood before his five new shirts, and choose the light grey with blue pin stripe. The mirror said it all; classic but somewhat sexy with the new slim fitting slacks. He nodded, grabbed his keys, turned and gave himself a splash of cologne, then was off to the condos.

Sydney had the stove under control. The shrimp was prepared for sautéing, the linguini ready for the pot, and the salad, a gourmet delight. The doorbell rang.

She stood before the mirror for just a second, approving the slim lines of her skirt that barely reached her knees, and the off one-should black blouse accented with a single, nestling string of pearls. All was ready, and the look she received from El Chano was confirmation itself, as was the look she gave him.

"As handsome as all get-out," she breathed to herself. "Please, come in, I have your favorite ale."

Conversation glided easily around the tedious job of creating a home again. "Yes," she sighed, "where do you begin? Clothes can be a chore, but refurnishing your whole life is another. Isn't anything salvageable?"

"I think so. Like you, I have chrome and glass bookcases and tables that should be retrievable. My tastes lead more to to the contemporary. I particularly like your white sectional and was wondering what a massive grey tufted job would look like. I have art that lends itself to any décor. Wow, I am actually getting into it. Thanks. I also think a diversionary shopping trip would be enjoyable. Game?"

Sydney nodded her head. "I have Friday off, and I also know the buyer at Spencer's. She is a long-time friend and could probably tell you about every grey sectional in the country. Come on, time to sauté the shrimp. You can watch the linguini."

Meanwhile, down at headquarters, an extremely nervous Lieutenant stared at the clock. "Forty-five minutes and I haven't even showered." He ran out the door, ignoring his name over the speaker.

He knew it took exactly 10 minutes to his apartment, three to the 4th floor, and another 20 to get showered and dressed. That just left 12 minutes to get down to the car and over to her apartment. "Ha!" he said, as he sprinted down the stairs, flew in the car, and put up the flashing red light. "I do have an advantage," he smiled to himself.

He approached the last block and decided to have some fun. He put on the siren. As he pulled up and looked at the clock, it was 45 minutes to the second. The whole building was looking down at him but, he saw only her looking back at him. He got out and waved. "Quite an entrance," he chuckled. "Sometimes time and position can be used to one's advantage."

This time he decided on the elevator; no more need to hurry. Instead, he brushed any imaginary speck from his shoulders, and smoothed back his chestnut hair. His father may have been from Spain, but his beautiful mother was from the Netherlands, complete with those deep blue eyes that she passed on to her 6' 3" son.

He hoped the champagne, left over from the holiday's, wasn't shaken up too much; took it out of the bag that he hastily tossed in the receptacle, and pushed the button.

When he got out, she was standing in the hallway, hands on her slender hips, her blue dress cut to a deep "V" and the full skirt, still in motion around her knees.

Her face was red with either or both indignation and pleasure. He hoped it was more of the latter.

"You do know the whole building now knows I am either dating an important arm of the police or have possibly just robbed the First National."

As he got closer, her arms opened wide to receive him, and he did due diligence to the embrace, and decided to capitalize on the moment, and place a sound kiss on those beautiful pale, pink lips.

They stepped in and he stood, just inside the door, looking around at her home. The apartment was the same size as his, but looked so much larger and more comfortable. At the far end by the window was a medium size dining table with four chairs. Leaving space for traffic there was a couch strategically placed facing the far wall where a large TV was the only decoration. Two other chairs flanked the couch with an assortment of tables and lamps, all from the Louis the 15th era. The artwork was limited to one wall, and was mostly copies of Ruben and Rembrandt. The sofa was a soft dove-grey and the chairs picked up the scheme with oranges and greens. He liked it, and nodded his approval.

She smiled, and ushered him over to the larger chair. "Where are we going," she asked, as she went in search of her wrap.

"Going?" he chocked. She disappeared around the corner as he pulled out his cell and speed dialed Alex's. He had repocketed the phone as she entered the room, her eyes bright with anticipation. "I'm ready!"

Alex knew Bob's favorite table and escorted the couple to the only one marked reserved in the far corner, almost hidden by two palms. The sound of a violin floated from across the room, and Stella was enchanted. Bob smiled as he saw her face light up. He had requested they serenade the couple at least three times during the evening, and this would be the first.

There were two violins. The musicians were dressed in black with red cummerbunds;' their face in a perpetual smile, their music, one can only say, came from the soul. "Romance Incorporated," was the aura they gave with every stroke of the bow.

The Champaign had already been poured, and Stella held her glass in mid-air as the musicians - came closer. She was enchanted.

Bob raised his glass and gave a toast just as they reached the table, "To the most beautiful woman I have ever had the honor sharing a bottle of champagne."

She smiled, and they both sipped. The music drowned out everything but the admiration they had for each other. It was the beginning of a beautiful evening.

The music played on and their eyes were the only way they could speak to each other. It was magical.

By the time the musicians moved on, they had to begin conversation again and at first it was difficult. The words were slow to come, full of the moment of romance.

Bob knew it was time to think of food. Sometimes it was up to the man to move things forward.

"Stella, if you agree, I highly recommend the veal, unless your taste runs to chicken, and then I suggest the parmesan.

"The veal Marsala, of course."

The salads arrived, as did the second bottle of champagne. Bob wondered about her capacity, but so far, she appeared in control.

The conversation was light and complimentary. Each one still looked approvingly into the others eyes. Bob was more than confident that this evening might end up in a very desirable place.

They were mid-way through the veal when he felt the vibration of his cell phone in his pocket.

"Damn," he said under his breath. He looked up at Stella and shook his head. "So, sorry. I guess I have to take this." He slid it open and discovered the face of Luis glaring at him.

"Boss, sorry to bother you, but we have, um, a little problem down at the Mexican restaurant.

"Problem! What could be so important that you would have to bother me. I am out with the most beautiful woman and . . . "

"Boss, there's been another murder!"

Chapter 9

Here We Go Again

"I'm coming too!" announced Stella, as Bob hastily told her of the murder and beckoned Alex for the check.

"This is a murder investigation," he argued. "I don't want you to get hurt."

"Hurt? The murder has already happened, and besides, I can help with the staff. They know me."

"All right, but keep a low profile and please, be discrete."

She smiled at the 'discrete' part, but jumped in the car beside him as they sped through town with sirens blaring and light flashing. She loved it, and he saw the excitement in her face.

"This is one hell of a date," she smiled. "I wonder what's for desert?"

Bob smiled back, only because he knew desert was not going to be what he was anticipating.

Luis was waiting at the entrance, and his eye-brows went up when he saw Stella come in with Bob, along with the instructions to go to the kitchen and 'just engage in casual conversation.'

"Wait a minute," he yelled, "that's where the body is.

They stopped in their tracks. "Where is it, actually?" asked Bob.

"It's in the walk-in freezer. And the kitchen staff is sitting at the celebrity table and the patrons are gathered there, on the other side of the dining room. Stella took off for the table as Bob and Luis rushed to the kitchen. The team had not arrived yet, so in the half-glow of the kitchen, the space took on a ghostly atmosphere. Shapes became distorted, the aprons hanging on the wall looked like they were about to attack and grab one of the butcher knives displayed on the wall behind; the large mixing bowl that looked like the cook preparing the heads of the soux-chefs. Even the harmless pots and pans became lethal weapons.

"Look out Luis, everything takes on a sinister shape at night, especially near a murder scene. Now where is the freezer, and who am I expecting to see inside?"

"It's Juan El Soro, the California agent for Clare, our last victim."

"Juan," commented Bob, his head cocked to one side. "I seem to remember he wasn't very talkative. One of those guys who was never really sure of who or what he really saw. Now we will never know unless there is enough of him left to talk."

"Sorry, boss, this guy is really dead. There's an ice pick, almost the size of a lance that skewered him to the wall. That's not all, we are back in heavy bleeding. I am not taking to this case at all. Whoever the killer is, his tastes run too much to the macabre for me."

"Seems like another blood bank was robbed. It will be interesting to see if the blood type matches." Bob stared up at the corpse. "How the hell did he get the guy to stand still for that skewering? Talk about macabre; this is more like Frankenstein meets Dracula."

The noise outside signaled the arrival of the team. "Well, Doc's here. It will be interesting to see how he reacts to this one. He said he was getting bored. Bored, hell."

"Hey Doc, come on in. It's a little chilly, but what the hell, chances are, the guy who did this is will never be cold in this life or the next."

Doc smirked and shook off the cold. "I have had a lot of barbecues in my lifetime, and done a lot of kabobs, but I would never know where to look for a skewer that size."

"Must be some commercial size for doing a half dozen of anything at one time," smirked Bob. "The boys will find out where he got it.

Doc gave the remains a quick once over. The cold was beginning to get to everyone. Luis was actually starting to jump up and down. Bob just wrapped his arms around himself and grunted, "Can't we hurry the process, Doc, I'm turning blue."

Doc stood back for one final look. "I don't like the looks of his tongue, but can see no other entry wounds at this time. I can finish with him in the lab. Let's get the hell out of here.

They left to allow the rest of the forensic team to get to work, "Sorry boys," said Doc., "at least the evidence is well preserved" he snickered. Doc's humor is often weak, this time it wasn't even acknowledged.

Once outside, Bob gave instructions to his team, as they were about to interview the patrons. "Come on," yelled Bob, "coffee on me; we need a conference."

Five minutes later, Bob, Luis and Doc sat in their now familiar booth in the coffee shop down the street. Bob spotted just one jelly donut under the glass on the counter and claimed it. Luis and Doc didn't seem to mind the two maple bars nestled beside it. However, it was the coffee; hot and steaming, that they held lovingly in their hands, that brought on the smiles.

"Now, down to business," said Bob as he pulled out his pad. Two main things I want to run by you two. One, did either of you notice the dolly that was under the table by the back door just down from the freezer. Second, did you happen to see that the frozen strawberries were mixed in with the bags of frozen jalapenos?"

"Who the hell is going to look at jalapenos when we have a corpse harpooned to the wall," complained Doc.

"Wait a minute, Doc, that's how Bob got to be Lieutenant; he notices things, and believe it or not, boss, I did notice the dolly, thinking at the time, what an awkward place to store it.

"I did not notice the strawberries or the dolly, and that's probably why I am just a doctor. "But, for now, I am going to see what the team may have seen," and he waved as he marched out the door, leaving Bob to pay for the coffee and donuts.

"How do you like that guy" smiled Luis, "he didn't even leave a tip."

"I didn't expect him to. It's a little game we play. I buy, he buys, but we always seem to know what the tally is. I am pretty sure he pays for the next one. You'll see, it just happens that way."

"I think I'll go back and see how Stella is doing with her new under-cover assignment," smiled Bob. "Somehow, I feel she will be pretty good at it. And how about you check on the dolly for me. Seems like an unlikely place to store one, unless, of course, it was just recently used to transport something heavy and awkward"

Luis shook his head as they walked back to the restaurant. "How do you do it boss? This is the third case we have worked together where you seem to find some good looking babe to hook up with."

"Not true, Luis. If you remember Donna, she went back to her fiancée just days after the case closed. Seem like my liaisons never last. Guess I don't have staying power. I was beginning to lose all self-esteem."

Luis held his sides as he burst out laughing. "You, boss, no self-esteem? No way, Jose. Anyway, seems to me that you and Stella are pretty compatible."

"I've thought so before, Luis. I have been wrong so many times, I really have lost my edge, whatever that is."

Doc came running into the dining room when he spotted Bob. "Damn, you were right. I had the boys check the dolly, and sure enough there were traces of blood. How did you know?"

"Elementary, my dear. . . "

"Don't you dare call me Watson. I'll give you the Sherlock on this one, but I'm still my own man."

"No question about that, Doc; now, how about the jalapenos?"

"Right again, that is if you can guess what they were used for. Seems like a lot of the frozen fruits and vegetables were used, as many more were out of place. But why"

"To keep the body cool, of course," said Bob, trying not to sound too annoying. Another example of the conjurors trick of trying to bamboozle the audience, or the police, in this case."

Bob exited before anyone could comment anymore, and went in search of Stella. He found her sitting at the bar all alone sipping on something tall and frothy.

"How did you get that umbrella drink? The restaurant is supposed to be closed. We've got a dead guy in the back"

"Hold on," she defended. "I interviewed every customer and my throat was dry." She pulled out a small notebook, "See, I even took notes which I will type on my computer tonight and email them to you directly. And the drink is from my friend, Jake, the bartender over there. He's a good friend of mine. Don't go looking like that. I said 'friend,' and that is what I meant. The only man I am involved with is standing right here, glaring at me with unhealthy thoughts,"

Bob shook his head. "You're right. Absolutely right. I have to learn when to turn off the detective. It's a bad habit, sorry!"

"Sorry? I haven't heard that word in quite a while. Here, have a sip, it will do you good."

"It's getting late," he smiled. "I had better take you home.

Imagine, I just had a jelly donut with Doc and Luis. I am losing it."

Bob looked sheepishly over at Stella, which brought out her softer side. She slid down from the stool, walked over, put her arms around his neck, and gave him the biggest kiss he could ever remember having without any encouragement from him, what-so-ever.

"Come on, take me home," she whispered.

Well, just for the reader's curiosity. Bob's former apprehension about the evening ending poorly vanished. Once they reached her apartment, they were arm in arm.

"Are you hungry?" she asked. And as soon as she asked the question, she wondered why she asked it. She knew food was the farthest thing from each of their minds. Yes, she was attracted to this big hulk, but was tonight the night?

She walked over and put her hands around his neck. "We are both tired. How about some bacon and eggs, and then resume this thought when we are fresher on another night. What do you think?"

Bob was finding it hard to breathe, his emotions were getting the better of him, and he knew she was right, He sure didn't want their first encounter to be dragged down by exhaustion.

"Don't look so forlorn, all that food we had as well as the jelly donut is long gone. Breakfast, then home to bed, to fight another day," she laughed out loud.

He joined her in the laughter and spread out on the couch to await his peace offering before bed. "Yep, she's right," he nodded to himself. "Next time."

Then he remembered, he hadn't called El Chano to bring him up to date. After all, they were now co-investigators on this case. He grabbed his phone and dialed

"El Chano, ready for some news? We have had another murder down at the Mexican restaurant. Yes, you can believe it. How about meeting me there in the morning. Yes, I'll have the coffee. No donuts. See you then."

He walked over to the table where breakfast was now being served. He was feeling a little too comfortable. He looked over at Stella and liked very much what he was looking at.

"Yes, I could take a lot of this," he thought to himself.

The next morning the closed sign was up in front of the restaurant. "Tough on business," commented El Chano, as he and Bob walked to the front door, each holding a steaming cup of coffee.

It was only 8:00 but the restaurant was already buzzing with activity. Doc came swishing out of the kitchen, his white coat flapping in his wake. "Damn, he said, "All those frozen vegies kept the body cool just to aggravate my blood pressure and confuse the time of death." He turned to Bob, "You worked that one out, didn't you?"

Bob took the compliment. "Yeah, I figured he was killed someplace else; that skewer had to be pounded through him while he was lying down. I figure he was already dead when they took the mallet down off the wall above the chopping table, and hammered away, I figure he was slipped a Mickey or maybe fentanyl to either kill him or bring him to the edge."

Doc ran inside the kitchen and dashed to the chopping table with Bob and El Chano on his heels.

Yes, there was a mallet hanging next to the carving knives. Doc put on his gloves and carefully took it down and placed it on a plastic sheet. Then, with the magnifying glass, poised for 30 seconds from the lethal end, he let out a grunt.

"Bob, you amaze me sometimes. If I didn't know better, I would think you looked pretty suspicious, yourself. Uh, uh, don't you say it."

"You mean 'elementary,' my good man,'" smiled Bob, taking the best Sherlock pose he could muster, and using his pen as a prop for the famous corn cob pipe.

"I see it," said El Chano. I can't see the victim being harpooned to the wall alive. I suppose that would account for the dolly being haphazardly placed under that table over there."

Doc threw up his hands and left the kitchen, yelling as he went, "Now everyone is a detective."

"Anything else?" asked El Chano, as he walked over to the freezer. May I look at the frozen bags used for keeping the damn fool from telling us when he died. By the way who has an alibi that would necessitate the cool-down."

"That was next on my agenda. Hey, what did you find? The boys went over this place with a fine tooth."

"Over here," said Chano, "there's a foot print in the blood. Hell of a lot of blood again."

"Yeah, and the foot print has the same tread as one of the forensic guy's sneakers. Saw it myself."

"Yes but, what if?"

"What if, what?"

"What if that was not the only pair of similar bloody treads running around here. It just could be that the killer finally slipped up. I know I've seen that particular patten before. I even know the brand name."

Bob thought for a moment. "I'll give you this one. I can easily see that happening. However, this killer is no dummy. Chances are his sneakers are as clean as a whistle right now."

I have heard it said," continued El Chano, "that blood is the hardest thing to hide. Don't you have special lights to pick up even the smallest trace?

Bob nodded "But I just can't go out and gather up all the sneakers from everyone that was close to or in the building around the time of the murders.

"No, I see that," said El Chano "but as the investigation continues you can certainly include it in your routine."

Bob nodded, and went in search of Luis. "You'll make a detective, yet, he called back, over his shoulder.

El Chano decided to stay and poke around by himself.

He stopped one of the forensic crew and asked if they knew where the dolly was normally housed.

"I am just going out there. It's a shed around back. Come on"

El Chano followed the name tag that read Maurice outside through the kitchen rear door, and onto a large paved area with a shed next to the clump of rhododendrons on the other side.

"We have finished here, so you don't have to be careful. Anyway, the gardener said he kept the dolly in the shed because everyone used it to hall in boxes and other food products. The delivery truck only has one dolly and when they used two they got the job done faster."

The shed was not secured, the combination lock hung opened on the metal latch. First, he walked around the outside, and through the adjacent rhododendron that seemed a natural place to hide or bury something that you never wanted found. Why did he think that, he wondered. He took a stick and started moving the leaves around. Somehow, he had the eerie feeling that he was standing in the place where two murders had been committed.

"Now I wonder why I feel so strongly about that? They say when you are in the presence of evil the hairs on the back of your neck stand up." They were standing. Not only that, he actually felt his flesh crawl.

El Chano was a good six feet away from the shed where the leaves were thicker. He moved closer to the bushes. By now, he could feel beads of sweat run down his temples. He brushed against the bushes and noticed that the leaves were more disturbed here than in the other areas. He started moving them around with his foot. Yes, he could see that the ground beneath had been disturbed.

"More than disturbed," he whispered to himself. "It's a different color."

He took out his handkerchief and scooped up a slice of earth. He folded it gently and placed it in his pocket. He continued to look and something shiny caught his eye over to the right. From where he stood it looked like a ring and he was about to bend over to pick it up when something dark and heavy came down on his head and plunged him into that proverbial black hole.

Bob had finished talking to the staff and went in search of El Chano. He met Maurice in the kitchen hall and asked him if he had seen Chano

"He is quite the sleuth now," he commented. "I took him out to the shed," and he pointed through the back kitchen door."

Bob followed his direction and started to run when he saw the huddled shape beneath the rhododendron. He found a pulse and dialed 911.

"He saw something," Bob whispered. "Nobody could just sneak up on him without his putting up a fight. He had to have been bent over, maybe to pick up something." He was about to walk away when he heard the sirens, and at the same time he caught a glimpse of a shiny object.

"That must be it," he said excitedly, as he reached over to retrieve it just as the paramedics came wheeling the gurney through the leaves.

"I'll ride with him, if you don't mind," asked Bob, as he climbed in beside his old friend and held on as they sped off, sirens blaring. After all, the police Lieutenant was on board.

Bob took the ring out of his pocket, now nestling his handkerchief. "Probably no fingerprints, but we can't take any chances."

It was a class ring, He thought it looked like college, and he was sure he had seen it before, or at least one like it. The filigree was hard to read but it seemed to be USC. Oh, boy, he whistled. I know about six buddies from USC. Of course it could have been the victims. Definitely wasn't Clare's. Unless. . ."

El Chano still had not woken up by the time they reached the hospital. Bob jumped out the back of the ambulance and they quickly pulled out the gurney, lowered the legs, and ran him into emergency. They were ready for him and took him right into the MRI room, Bob was left cooling his heels, or rather pacing in front of the nurses station, driving them all crazy.

"Lieutenant!" called out the buxom nurse, "we have a coffee lounge right around the corner. How about waiting there. I personally will come and get you the moment he returns.'

Before he could leave, one of the doctors walked up to him and held out his hand, "We found this in his pocket. It looks like something that is more in your line than ours."

Bob opened the handkerchief, and glared at a slice of dirt. Not just any dirt, he could see, but dirt saturated in blood.

He speed dialed Luis, and asked him to hurry over to Mercy General. "Luis, El Chano found some important clues, but he is out for the count. Need you here, ASAP."

Bob found the coffee, but knew it had been steeping all day, so he dumped it. Then he started pacing again, just as the buxom nurse came through the door.

"Lieutenant, Mr. El Chano has been moved up to room 307 and is now conscious. The nurse said you may see him."

Bob sprinted for the elevator and grabbed a chocolate cake off the tray in the hallway. He stood quietly before 307. Not a sound. Then a nurse came bustling out with tray in hand. "If you are Bob, you had better go in. He is having a conniption.'"

Bob sheepishly walked through the door. "Hay buddy, I think you will make detective of the year. Is this what you were looking for when thy clobbered you?"

El Chano held out his hand and took the ring. "Sure looks like it. Hard to tell for sure with this pounding headache. All I know for sure is there was something shinny that looked like a ring. I was concentrating on that and not some would be assailant that was about to clonk me over the head. And, no, I didn't even get a glimpse of him"

"Sorry, my amigo. Isn't there something you can take for that pain?"

"They already have me on oxi something, and it will be a couple of hours before I get another dose. Hey, what about the dirt I picked up?"

"Another winner, the lab just called on my cell and verified that it was blood. Now, we will find out who it belonged to. I think we both know the answer that one, Thanks, Chano, for a good piece of detective work. I don't know why our team didn't cover a larger area in their search."

"I always had it in the back of my mind that Clare had to have been killed on the premises, close enough to get her in position during the time frame the killer created to give himself an alibi. At least, that's the only reason I can see for all the drama. Well, one of the reasons, anyway. I suppose the shell game you are always talking about is to get us to watch one hand while the other palms the evidence. I am wondering what Juan saw that got him killed? Probably saw the killer palm something." He tried to laugh but ended up holding his head. "Hurts too much."

"I think you are right on, Chano. One of my men told me that Juan was seen asleep at the celebrity table just before they packed up and left. What if, after the team left, out killer didn't see Juan and went after a piece of evidence in the dining room."

"Yeah," said Chano, "and what if, just as he retrieved it, Juan opened his eye and saw everything. That could have sealed his fate, right then and there. Or, what if it reminded him of what he had seen earlier; say when the snakes were slithering about. I think that is when the actual evidence was retrieved. Your boys would have seen it earlier. Elementary, dear Watson. "

"OK, I'll give you this one, Sherlock. I hate to play Watson"

"Oh, damn, I want more pain meds. I'm not a wimp, Bob, but this really hurts." He pushed the button, and the buxom nurse came in holding a small tray with juice and a plastic cup.

"OK, darlin,' here we are. Time for that pill and for all visitors to leave so you can get some rest.

They waved their goodbyes and Bob headed downstairs to find a much-needed fresh cup of coffee.

Chapter 10

The Old Alma Matter

Bob slid into the booth and gazed out at the garden surrounding the cafeteria. He felt badly about El Chano, and secretly believed that the killer was toying with them.

"There is no earthly reason to conk Chano over the head, especially with that lead pipe Luis found just feet from the scene. Lead pipe, damn. I can't wait to get my hands on that thug. One thing I have found, though," he whispered to himself, "when a killer gets this sure of himself, he usually messes up."

He went back for a second cup and gazed out at the gardener who was raking around the rose bushes. "Hmmm," he pondered, "doesn't the restaurant have a gardener; seems long over due for some work in the back. Of course, it's the back and not the front where the grounds need to be more manicured. I wonder?"

He pondered his new thought for a minute, then took out the ring that was still secure in his handkerchief. He watched the red garnet sparkle in the sunlight.

"This had to be an oversight, Seems like Juan had to be a CSU graduate, or purchased a ring for business reasons. Then there is Clare, but why would she be wearing a ring? I didn't know the woman personally, but she sure doesn't sound like a grad to me."

Bob gently folded the ring back up and placed it in his pocket. He picked up his cell and dialed. "Luis, take your suspect list and see if any of them went to CSU. See if there are any grads. I know this is a long shot but give it a try. If you have any luck, get me. I am not going to leave any stone unturned, or in this case, a ring unturned. If you come up with any give me a call and I will pop over the grape vine and make visit." Bob took the elevator back up to thr 3rd floor and peeked into Chano's room.

"I see you boss. Please come in, I am bored silly. You have the look of the cat who swallowed the canary. What's up?"

"I have a hunch about that ring you saw when you were conked over the head. The killer must have known it was in the vicinity and knew it would come back to haunt him. There is a year engraved in the filigree that would help identify him, especially if that was the year he graduated. I am having Luis check our list to see if there are any CSU students among them. If so, I am buzzing back to my alma matter."

"You too, amigo? Wouldn't it be something if you two even took classes together."

"Ha, maybe even studied criminology together."

"That would explain why he is so smart," laughed Chano, "Sorry Bob, couldn't resist."

The cell rang and it was Luis. "Hey boss, I have three names. Go figure. Are you going over?"

"First I am going to stop there for pictures then be on my way. This could be our first real break, thanks to our good friend here with the bandage on his head. Be right down; hope we photographed everyone. No, I don't like showing pictures of dead men, or women, for that matter, but I will if I have to."

Bob would have made better time if he hadn't stopped at the outlets for a couple of shirts, and a new pair of slacks. After all, a Lieutenant, and head of criminal investigation doesn't live by crime alone. There were dates, and who knows what, coming up with Stella; his appearance needed a boost. At least he thought so. However it was just after 2:00 when he rolled up in front of the administration building, He showed his police badge through the plastic, and breezed inside. He showed the list to the first gal he saw, and she escorted him to a desk down the hall in a cubical. Once inside he laid out his list and the pictures.

"I need to compare these with your records. It's important. We have had two homicides, and I am afraid of what our killer might want to do next. I need your help. He also placed the ring on the desk.

She looked up at him and smiled. It was the plea for help that did it. She reached over and picked up the ring. "I just love the garnet in this ring. The gals love it too if they should be lucky enough to wear one around their neck. Oh, look here, on the inside. Seems like someone did wear it around her neck; see how the chain has scratched the inside. Hmmm, seems like its quite worn. Well, that's your department, Lieutenant. Let's look at those pictures."

She spread them out and took her time. She looked at the two with their eyes closed and looked back at the Lieutenant. "Victims?"

He nodded.

"Neither of them are familiar. The names are foreign too, but I will check them with our records. She must have been beautiful; maybe a little hard around the edges."

She typed in the names and got an immediate response. "Here they are. Oh, look, there is another three that are not on your list. How about that. And there you are, Lieutenant, and is this a relative by the name of Marko who came three years behind you?"

"Yeah, that is my baby brother, he is a Colonel now. By the expression on your face it must say something about his repeated skirmishes on campus."

"I would say more than skirmishes. During the panty raid, one of the girls actually fell out of her window, but all ended well."

Bob shook his head. "Didn't hear all of that. My apologies are worthless, but you have them anyway."

"Now, I would like to know what that glint in your eye means. You see something, don't you? Who is the other dude."

"It's the picture, and not the name. He went here, all right, but one of these names is an alias. I wonder which one?" she asked.

Bob couldn't stand it. He rose and walked behind her chair and glared at the picture "Well I'll be damned! Is there anyway I can get a print-out of all his records. I would like to find something to help nail him to the wall. Oh, and a print-out of all the others, too. You have no idea how much help you have been. "

The clerk was noticeably pleased and promised his request would be completed in about half an hour.

"I'll just walk around campus. Take your time, and thanks again for your detective work."

Once outside, Bob drew in a deep breath of fresh air. He scratched his head and headed for a bench that once was an all too familiar place to study for exams. He always preferred the outdoors to the stuffy dorms or the small apartment he shared with his roomey. "Ah, those were the days. Or were they? No glory days because he never had anything to boast about. He just made it through with a solid 3.4, which was good enough to get him into Lieutenant's school. He got up and started walking to the old dorm. "So long ago, now," he sighed. He thought of the girl he dated for two years and wondered where she was today.

"Can't go back, can't go back. She started dating that pre-med ass. I didn't stand a chance." He shook his head and wandered back. No point walking the three blocks to the apartment. "It was just a place to crash, after all." He sighed again and as he entered the door of administration the clerk was holding a large manila envelope, and grinning from ear to ear.

"It has been a pleasure to serve you, sir. Here is my card. Don't hesitate to call if there is anything else you need."

Needless to say, the trip back went quickly. Bob's head was literally spinning. "Now what?" he shouted out loud. "It is certain I can't act on any of this information. Hell, not yet, anyway. Have to keep it under my hat until the right moment. Then BAM!!!"

He asked his phone to dial Stella. She answered. "It's Bob. I'm coming back from the coast with evidence and would love to share dinner and champagne with you tonight. Great! See you at 7:00 PM."

He was feeling better already.

Chapter 11

More Romance Anyone?

Just about anyone would tell you that if you are looking for romance stay out of the hospital. Well, maybe not everyone.

Bob decided to pop by to see El Chano before he headed home. No it was too soon to share the day with him. Maybe in a couple of days, or sooner, if some of his hunches panned out.

As he approached 307, he heard voices. Not wanting to intrude he stood outside and waited. All was silent for a moment so he decided to venture in. Wrong move. As he entered, he caught Chano and one of the most beautiful women he had ever seen in a very passionate embrace. "Hmmm," he thought to himself, "those pain pills must have kicked in."

He kicked the door by mistake, and broke the lover's spell.

"So sorry Chano, wouldn't have interrupted for the world.

Sydney stood up, brushed her slacks and smiled coquettishly, which was hard to pull off. Chano reached over and grabbed her hand and gave it a squeeze. Their eyes met and said it all,

"Dinner, my place, tomorrow at 7:00 PM. See you." She blew them both a kiss and literally skipped out.

"Wow," said Bob, you can really pick them."

Chano nodded and stretched both arms as high as he could. "Tomorrow night can't come soon enough for me. Now, to what do I owe this visit?"

"I took a trip to USC and showed the pictures to administration. Too many people went to that school. However, I have my favorites. No, you'll have to wait a few before I tell you. Yes, to your unspoken question. I think we are a lot closer. I have more evidence to gather and may have to go out of town again. This person has a history in Palm Springs. I'm due for some R&R so I think maybe Monday. I was wondering if your head would be healed enough to go? There's no way we will leave before your dinner tomorrow; mine, for that matter, tonight. Believe it or not buddy, I have another round with the stunning Stella. This time I figured I would take her for Chinese at the Dragon's Lair. What do you think?"

"Only if you ask for El Chano's table. No, I am not saying a word. It will be my little surprise for you tonight.

Oh, and order the number 3 special and tell them to put it on my tab."

"OK buddy, I'll follow your lead. You heal your head so we can solve this case."

Bob quickly showered and surveyed his wardrobe. "I think I need to go shopping like Chano and get some new duds. He pulled out his blue shirt and fingered a tie, then shook his head. "Over the top. Maybe. He pulled out the blue and white stripe and held it up. I really think she'll like it. If I know her, she will dress up. I would like to meet the challenge."

Well, that's how it came about. The Homicide Lieutenant stood in front of his girl's door, complete with tie and, yes, you guessed it, a bouquet of flowers. She opened the door.

She was a vision in a pale blue dress with a low V-neck and sleeveless, to boot. She was speechless. Really speechless. Bob had to clear his throat to speak.

"Well, may I come in?"

She waved him in, still overcome by his grandeur, and said, "Are you going to propose tonight, or what. You are beyond gorgeous?"

Bob found himself actually blushing, but from somewhere, he knew not where, came his reply, "If I thought you would say yes, I would give it a try."

This time they both stood looking inquiringly at each other. "Tell you what," she finally said, "ask me again in a few weeks with the understanding of a long engagement, maybe 6 months."

Without realizing what he was doing, Bob actually nodded in agreement, followed by, "It's a deal." All the time secretly wondering how he was ever going to live through the next few weeks, let alone the rest of the evening.

They left for the Dragon and were pleasantly surprised by the special table that was always reserved for El Chano. The table was one of three on a two step up balcony surrounded by bamboo and palms. They found themselves seated in the furthest corner, quite secluded from the rest of the patrons.

"This is beyond seductive," smiled Stella. "I have never dined with so much atmosphere; it is absolutely dripping."

Bob nodded, as the waiter, all in black except for the white towel draped over his arm holding a bottle of champagne, with two glasses in the other hand. "Compliments of El Chano, as is the entree. He called to give us the order, if you approve. We began with the duck over an hour ago, so your wait will not be so long."

"Friends! What would we do without them? And now, with your permission, I would like to make a toast."

Stella beamed. "By all means," and she raised her glass.

"To the most beautiful woman that I have ever had the pleasure of proposing." They clicked, and he continued, "And I am fortunate to sit across from you and gaze into those deep, green eyes all evening."

It would have been a toss-up for any on-looker at that moment. As their eyes met, the blush that rose from Bob's tie was almost as red as the one on Stella's cheeks.

"If this is love," thought the waiter, as he poured another glass of champagne, we had better turn on the air-conditioning."

The second bottle of champagne sat on the table, and by now the couple was actually holding hands across the table-cloth. Conversation mostly centered around bits and pieces of eachother's life story, starting from around age five and ended up at high school graduation before the duck arrived. It was spectacular, and Bob felt that anything he could do to repay his buddy, would pale in comparison.

The second bottle was now empty, as were their plates, when the waiter magically appeared again. "El Chano just called from his hospital bed and said to tell you to enjoy the rest of the evening, and to say that he hoped your evening was as romantic as he always remembered."

The ride home was quiet; what can be said after the most perfect evening each one had experienced. Once they stood in front of her door, she moved very slowly fumbling for her key. Each one needed time to think.

"I have no champagne," she said feebly, "but I can make coffee. That is the one thing you miss at a Chinese restaurant."

"Coffee would be great," said Bob, thankful that he didn't have to think of something to get inside. However, once inside the door, her purse on the table, and her wrap on the couch, the pot never got filled.

Bob was not completely with out a move or two. He quickly encircled her waist and drew her to him. She folded in his arms easily, and the next thing they both knew her hands wrapped around his neck and she was on her toes, straining to reach his height and the lips that were waiting for hers.

Two long kisses later found them both grouping for each other, and moving more quickly, now toward the door on the other side of the kitchen.

Once inside, her shoes went flying, as did his necktie, lost in the shadows on the other side of the bed that was quickly being unwrapped. The clothes were now scattered about the floor, leaving two breathless bodies totally immersed in each other.

It would be indiscrete to record any conversation after this point for it would be totally undiscernible.

About 10:00 the next morning, El Chano stood before Bob's desk, almost like he was back in the army at attention before his CO. "Reporting for duty sir! Doc said I could return to the front lines in two days. Is that soon enough to join you in battle?"

Bob stood up, pleased to see his old friend in the vertical. He gently clasped his shoulders. "Perfect; I thought we would fly to Palm Springs. It is just under an hour, and will probably take a couple of days to poke around. Say, mi amigo, last might was amazing. I don't know how to thank you. All I can say is I accidently proposed."

"What? How in the world do you 'accidently propose? You either do or you don't. Come on, amigo. Let loose."

Bob let loose, and it left both of them holding their sides and laughing. "So now," continued Bob, "I have to tough it for a couple of weeks and ask again. Whew, don't know if I'll make it."

"Well, if you do, just be sure you are in your right mind. Serious stuff, mi amigo. Just follow your heart, they say. I have often come close, but never made it to the alter. If you do, I hope you will consider me standing next to you. I have never been a best man, either."

"You are turning me into a blithering idiot, Chano. Come on, coffee is on me."

That night, as Chano stood at Sydney's door, Bob's experience from the night before flashed through his mind, and he couldn't help but wonder if the beautiful woman on the other side of the door could be his next date at the Dragon.

"I understand you like Chinese," she smiled as she ushered Chano to the white couch. He almost blushed. "Can you drink, or are you on meds?"

"I am over the meds, and Bob and I are leaving for Palm Springs on Thursday to do a little sleuthing together. I really like that guy. I think I'll be best man at his wedding."

"Wow. When will that be?" she asked, as she handed him an ale.

"Well, from what he said, he has to propose again in a couple of weeks, and then there is to be a long engagement. I give them a month." They both burst out laughing, and she usherd him to the couch. One seated, with their drinks on the table, and the aroma of the roast teasing their appetite, El Chano wasted no time. Sydney was in his arms and the kisses were long and sweet.

"Must be something in the air," he whispered to himself.

Chapter 12

Palm Springs and Beyond

Bob was always in a quandary about how much to pack for a three or four day trip, especially to an area where the temperature was recorded in the three digits. "That's the deciding factor," he said out loud to his suitcase. "I know I'll need more than the usual pair of slacks and daily shirt and underwear. There's no staying power for anything, especially slacks or shorts. He decided to wear one pair of shorts, pack two, and one pair of slacks.

The shirts were easy and consisted of three knits and one Hawaiian. Even dinner and gambling at the Crazy Horse Casino would do justice to his grey and grey.

"Well, a guy has to have a little fun if he can, and this time it will run only to gambling. Hope El Chano is of the same mind. No time or desire, for that matter, to be on the prowl."

Before he knew it, he pulled up in front of Chano's hotel, and there he was, looking as sharp as ever in his kaki's and black. "I'm really looking forward to this trip,

Bob," he said as he loaded his suitcase. Did you hear it was a hundred and three today. Sure made it hard to pack."

Bob nodded, and pointed the car towards the Bakersfield Airport where a King Air was waiting to take them to Palm Springs.

"Piece of cake," said Bob, "it will only take a little under an hour. The only problem is I would prefer to come over during early spring before the desert heats up."

"Well, it's not like we are going to trek around the desert looking for nuggets. I brought my suit, did you?"

Bob nodded, "Wouldn't forget that. I have to have some tan to show the ladies when we get back."

"Ho, ho," said Chano, "and how many would that be? An even dozen?"

Bob laughed, and gave Chano a look. "You know as well as I do there is only one I want to impress right now. Hope I can do it."

The chit-chat continued for a while until El Chano finally asked when he would be brought into the loop. "When are you going to tell me exactly why we are traipsing to the Springs? Or are you going to make me guess?"

"Guess?" asked Bob. "Do you think you can?"

"Maybe. Let's see if I am any good as a detective. How about I start with your trip to USC. You said you found a few matches. The three you named I easily discounted. Not smart enough. Now the third one I would like to try to guess." Chano took out his pad and wrote down a name. "Let's just leave it here," he said. When the trip is over, we'll see if I get the promotion, or not," he laughed.

Bob looked at the name and tried not to show any expression. "We'll see," he said. You may get the job after all."

"I can give you some background, though. The name I picked went to UNLV before he transferred to USC. I could see by the records that there was quite a review before they decided to admit him. He had what they called a blemished record."

El Chano laughed. "Blemished, huh? OK, tell me more."

At that time the school was experimenting with some new classes that they thought would bring in more revenue. The professor in the Geology department thought some hands-on studies would draw the students in, especially if it involved mining for GOLD,"

"Gold?" whistled Chano. "Now, you have peaked my interest."

"Not just yours, but they had at least 60 that signed up for the first semester. They really had to hustle, but they finally came up with a course study, if you can call it that. Two of the seniors majoring in Geology volunteered to go out into the desert and find a couple of 'died in the wool' miners to bring back for lectures. They also took the time to do a little mining of their own. Oh, they did their research. Would you believe there is quite a lot written on the subject, and every gold mine and claim, past or present, is listed as well on their productivity, or lack there of."

The boys did a good job; they not only found two old prospectors, but also came back with two nuggets valued at over $1500 dollars an ounce."

"I can tell you what happened next," said Chano. "That class filled up for the next two years."

"Ha, you're right," said Bob. "Now, there were no text books as yet, so they organized some print-outs from the internet that gave the history of mining in the area. Needless to say, it was almost like another gold rush."

"OK," said Chano, "is there any way we can cut to the chase?"

"If you insist," said Bob. "Now the two students we are using as our example, about to graduate at half term, were given early diplomas and were assigned to the department with pay."

"Pretty good gig, if you ask me," said Chano.

"I'll cut to the first field trip, because this is where the trouble begins. The prospectors plotted the first trip up to Ghost mountain and down through Dead Man's Gully. It is believed that a tributary once ran through there and supposedly left those black nuggets behind. The boys did not travel as deeply into the desert area as that, but the theory was that further up the dry river bank it just had to be more lucrative."

The class of '60 was divided into three excursions, with the professor leading one, and each boy with a prospector leading the others."

"Good grief, Bob, how long is this story going to be?"

"OK, the long shot of it is that one of the young leaders did not make it out alive. He was found with a prospectors hatchet buried in the back of his skull. At this point it is important to know that the three camps were only a mile or so apart."

"Were there nuggets found at this point?" asked Chano.

"You got it. According to group two, the one with the now dead geologist, had found one, which if divided between the 20 would equal around $1600 each"

"That's not enough for murder, is it?"

"Not that alone, but there is more. Supposedly that group also stumbled upon a cave off the track toward the mountain. It was here that the students believed their leader found enough gold to support them all for more than a lifetime."

"Who knew about the cave?"

"Only the dead man and the prospector who went exploring by themselves after the first nugget had been found. That very night it was reported that the two prospectors and the two boys were having a heated discussion over by one of the small campfires used to keep the wolves and coyotes away."

"The conclusion was not satisfactory, by any means. The prospectors were cleared because they lacked motive. After all there was enough in that gold mine to keep them all in luxury. With the boys, it was different. It seems that they argued about reporting the mine to the others. The survivor wanted to come back later to stake their own claim instead of making it a university find. That tore it, and the young geologist was arrested. That geologist is our present day suspect of two murders."

El Chano whistled. "So, how did he get away with it, if that is what he really did?"

"Lack of evidence, Watson, and to this day, the mystery goes unsolved. The surviving boy lost his diploma and was dismissed from the university. The prospectors were never able to find the mine again, and, of course, the whole 'hands on' project was abandoned."

OK, now bring me up to date," urged Chano. "What the hell are we going to Palm Springs for instead of Las Vegas?"

"Good question; answers after we arrive and settle."

The trip was smooth and under the hour estimation. The pilot was a long time friend of Bob's and was often used by the police department as their pilot. Flying Fred, needed to be fed.

Later, after checking in their motel, Chano just glared at Bob over his hamburger. "Where did you get all this information?"

"It's all on file at USC. They had to thoroughly examine the records to be sure they wanted to admit this would-be geologist who had been accused of murder. At first, they weren't going to, but it seems that a lawyer was hired that proved there was not enough evidence to keep a young man from getting his degree."

"But Palm Springs?" urged El Chano.

"After our suspect left Vegas he went to Palm Springs. After I got back from USC I checked with my computer and found that Mr Geologist had gotten into trouble, yet once again."

"You see, we figure he still had enough money from the first nuggets to begin prospecting again, so that is exactly what he did. Believe it or not, there are exactly 632 claims in the Palm Springs area, with 43 still active. Now, this is interesting, just in case you get the fever; there are 87 mines operating at the present time."

"Do any of those mines belong to our suspect?" asked El Chano.

"Bull's-eye! Yes, one mine, and four claims in all, but nothing big yet to our knowledge. ."

"I wish you had told me, I didn't pack any mining gear."

"No worries, I am renting a jeep, and all the equipment needed for a trek into the desert. Got it covered."

After dinner they returned to the Desert Sky Motel, showered down, and headed for the Crazy Horse, that was noted, not only for their gambling, but also for the best rib-eye in town. After all, that hamburger wouldn't last forever.

"Gamble first?" questioned El Chano.

Bob nodded. "I want to work up an appetite for that steak. What's your pleasure? Black Jack?"

They both headed over to the table and tested out their individual strategies. No one lost. El Chano appeared to be up around $150 before they decided to move on.

"No roulette for me," said Bob. "I can't afford to lose another shirt. How about some poker?"

El Chano perked up. "Now you're talking."

For the next hour they both sat, sober faced, playing the game that took more finesse than Black Jack. It paid off; by the time they rose to go to the dining room their fists were full of receipts to be cashed in. They nodded to each other, got their money and looked forward to a brew and their rib eye. It was a glorious day all around.

They had adjoining rooms so each one could jump into his own king size bed and dream about exploring the desert for black nuggets the next day. Oh, what a glorious night.

Chapter 13

. . . And Beyond

The jeep was delivered at the motel at 8:00 AM sharp, and was fully loaded with canteens of water plus a large plastic water container with a spit for easy pouring into the two tin cups. There was an assortment of camping gear for cooking as well as two bedrolls, and small tent.

Bob was pleased when he looked over the equipment and now it was up to him to secure the provisions that would fill the ice chest at the local general store, similar to a mini-mart.

El Chano appeared with his duffle bag and placed it in the rear of the jeep next to Bobs. They looked at each other, nodded, and drove the half block to pick up the food.

The proprietor was waiting for them, and he and an assistant loaded the chest onto the jeep.

"Everything you need. Eat the perishables first, and leave the canned meats for last. Also, if you need more food, in the wild, that is, l have included a knife that will prepare either rattle snake or rabbit. Very sharp."

Both Bob and El Chano grimaced, but graciously thanked the man for thinking of everything.

Bob took out his small county map and looked at the their first sign of real adventure; road number 78 that turned off highway 10, 9 miles south of town, "Once we turn off the highway we are in almost uncharted territory, I am turning the map over to you Chano, No GPS can help us now

They were both watching the speedometer because all the markings on the map were indicated in miles. The first was a left turn 41.6 miles from highway 10.

"I put the mileage meter on so we would not miss our turn."

Chano nodded and was anxiously watching the road as it became smaller and filled with more potholes.

"This jeep is a far cry from your SUV," laughed Chano. I actually have to hold on to stay vertical." They both laughed, and watched as the scenery became more like desert, and looking back they no longer could see any remnant of civilization.

"I see the hills up ahead," commented Bob, "and I am wondering if that will be the 41 mile mark. I am thinking it is because of the road that we are supposed to be traveling."

"Right," said Chano. "Look at the line on the map, it is barely a pencil line, and on top of that it seems to weave right up into those hills. What are we supposed to find up there?"

"There is supposed to be a working ranch owned by the Wilkies. Then, after we check in, and let them know we are passing through their property, we veer north along the ridge until we find a hill that looks like a mushroom."

"Good grief, Bob, are you telling me we are going to run out of road and have to depend on landmarks?"

Pretty much, that's why this may come in handy. Here, you can also hold the compass."

El Chano gaped at the small instrument in his hand and blinked "Bob, do you realize that this little bobble may mean the difference between life and death?"

"Yep," said Bob. "Kind of figured it might, but just between you and me, I sure hope it doesn't."

El Chano turned this way and that, watching the compass. I guess it works, but even if we know north from south how will we know which way to go?"

"The map, I guess," answered Bob. "I thought we might write down any more landmarks we see and their relationship to the rest of the terrain. The ranch will be the closest civilization. There are no towns. The further we get into those hills, the more isolated we become. We will be off ranch property, and as far as I know, it is open range. Actually that means, 'no man's land,.'"

"Are you still game?"

El Chano laughed. "Heck of a time to ask me that. What am I supposed to do, get out and walk?"

"Whoa, this is the 41 mile mark. Start looking for that road."

As bad as the road from town was, there was still a comfortable feel about it, that is, compared to the trail they just turned onto. A trail, only by name on the map, and marked by one post with an arrow pointing into the hills saying "Dead Man's Gulch."

"How the hell do we know when we are on the road at all?" asked Chano. Everything looks the same.?"

"Just barely, Chano. See, there are no rocks and no growth. If you look ahead there is kind of a line that weaves into the hills. It's hard to see, but this is all we have to go on. Fingers crossed. Keep your eyes glued."

No question about it, they were glued, watching every indication that there was actually a road under their wheels, and that they were actually heading somewhere.

"OK, Bob, tell me about Dead Man's Gulch. What are we supposed to find there?"

"That's part of our investigation. You see, our suspect has a mine located along the southern perimeter of the Gulch; not far from the mine there is supposed to be a cabin of sorts that will give us some shelter while we poke around."

"Poke around? What are we poking for? More bodies?"

"Possibly. He didn't go into this venture alone, and there is always the chance that old habits die hard."

"Good grief, is this guy some kind of a monster?"

"The thought has crossed my mind," agreed Bob.

It looked like they were about to rum out of road, if that is what they were on, when a pile of rocks loomed up ahead.

"Oh, oh, looks like they had an avalanche. What do we do now?"

"I am for looking to see if there is a way around that pile of rocks. I am not ready to abandon the jeep."

Bob got out and El Chano followed. However, they were back in the jeep with their boots held high.

"Look at that!" yelled Chano. "It's a sidewinder. Never saw one before. Look how fast he can travel. Let's wait until he is out of sight and hope he has a destination in mind, even though he doesn't seem to see where he is going."

They didn't have long to wait before the coast was clear and they both started exploring the rocks.

"Over here," yelled Bob. "I think if we move this rock I can get the jeep through. I have some rope that will help."

Bob got the rope and secured it around the rock, that was almost boulder size. The other end was tied to the rods at the rear of the jeep.

"You watch, Chano, as I slowly rev her up. And, stay clear; I don't want the rope snapping and taking you out."

"Hold on just a minute, Bob. Let me get that mini shovel I saw and clear away some of the sand in front of the rock."

He made as wide a path as he could when he heard a sound coming from the rock. He turned in time to see another rattler slither toward him.

"Rattler!" he yelled.

"Don't move!" ordered Bob as he drew his 38 and fired. The head was taken clean off and left the remains that didn't want to stop slithering, but finally did.

"Whew," said Bob. "I am sure glad it didn't ricochet.

Chano picked up some pebbles and threw them at Bob. "Get that damn rock out of here!"

And, he did.

There was now enough space to maneuver the jeep around the avalanche. On the other side of the hill Bob stopped the jeep.

"So this is what you call a gulch. I don't get it, but I suppose that old river bed down there represents the gulch, and beyond is just a valley enclosed by hills and mountains. OK, now look for something that represents a mushroom while I try to navigate this would-be gulch."

El Chano looked at the map and then at the horizon. "We've got to keep our bearings, you know Bob. I have a feeling that getting in here has been a piece of cake, but exiting may be a little harder. Hey, look over to the left. Doesn't that look like a mushroom on the top of that hill?"

"Right, now hold on while I try to get to the opposite bank."

Once they were again on flat ground, they both left the jeep and looked around. "One thing is for certain," said Bob. We can't depend on a road any more. It's landmarks all the way."

El Chano turned around and looked at the rocks and hills where they came through. "Bob, I am trying to remember that horseshoe shape over there, so if we ever try to get out of here, we know where to go."

They laughed together, but somewhere inside there was this prickly feeling of uncertainty. That 'if' was gnawing at both of them.

Once they were moving again Bob headed straight for the mushroom. "There is supposed to be a shack or something out here," he explained. At least we will have some protection."

"From what?" asked Chano. "As far as I can see there is nothing more menacing out here than a couple of sidewinders and a jack rabbit or two."

"Ho, ho," replied Bob. "Look up in those hills. There are mountain lions, as well as at least one pack of wolves. Coyotes, of course, but I haven't heard that they attack, unless starving."

"You are making my skin crawl," said Chano. "Hey, that looks like a shack over there. At least it is still standing,"

Ten minutes later they were both walking around the structure that was indeed a shack, for lack of a better name. They both felt the structure wasn't even fit for a backyard lawnmower.

There was no lock, so the door was easily creaked open as two furry, long tail critters scampered out. That wasn't all, the air was bad, and both thought that something had recently died here.

"Whatever that was, I hope it crawled out and found a burial ground somewhere else," commented Bob as he held his handkerchief over his nose.

No such luck, the prairie dog's remains were over by the single cot beneath the only small window in the tiny space. "Probably 6 x 6," said Chano. "I guess we can make this work, for a very short period of time, however.

Let's clean it up. Do we sacrifice some of our water to get the stench out of the floor? I vote yes."

"Yeah, some of that soap I brought, too. Let's leave the door open. The window looks operable. We need air."

With a tiny whisk broom, a pan of water and soap, a towel turned into a rag, and some elbow grease, it is amazing what was accomplished. The bed was stripped and the mattress hauled outside to air. The small wooden chair was washed and placed in the sun. A small rickety table, only big enough for one plate and one can of beer was also revived. The miniature potbellied stove was swept clean, and the window, freed from cobwebs and dust.

"Well, it's not exactly home sweet home," announced Bob, "but we have shelter."

"From what?" teased Chano again. "It is sure not likely to rain."

It was interesting how the night air cooled everything down, even their spirits. "We are going to have to take turns on the cot," said Bob. "The chair wasn't meant for sleeping, but I can prop it up against the shack and keep watch. We can take shifts."

It was agreed, so the boys unloaded some groceries and began to plan dinner. Well, plan would not exactly be the term they would choose. The decision on what can to open was quickly made, as was the decision NOT to hunt for their dinner. Bob had the foresight to ask for beer in the cooler, and they made quick work of four cans.

"Not too bad," complimented Chano, as he leaned back in the chair, propped against the wall. Bob chose to bring the jeep up close and lounge on the front seat with the top off."

"Nope, it's a lot like camping. Don't mind it a bit."

It didn't take long for the sun to dip behind the west hills and remind them that it would soon be as black as pitch.

"A fire!" yelled Chano. "Let's get cracking before we totally loose our light."

Once the dry, tumble-weed looking brush was neatly piled on top of some old roof shingles, sticks, and an unfired log propped against the shack, they had a fire. Just like home.

Chapter 14

You're Never Alone

They made it through the night. El Chano crashed on the cot while Bob managed to find a comfortable position in the jeep; not easy for his long-legged frame.

The sun peeked over the mountain, and two stomachs started to rumble. Bob headed toward the cooler and a frying pan. The fire was rebuilt, and before El Chano peeked out the door, the bacon was sizzling. They both smiled at the paper plates, but knew they would make good kindling for the next fire.

"Well?" said Chano, an inquiring tone in his voice,

"What are we really looking for? Do you think someone is buried around here?"

Bob savored the coffee he poured from the campfire pot, "Not bad for a novice," he smiled. "And, yes, I think that is what is out here. You see, we have a killer that has shown us his MO. He not only has no reservation about killing, he also has to build it into a theatrical setting. Drama, Chano, drama."

"If he really killed the geologist in Nevada, then I can see that he would repeat the deed here if it meant a big prize for him. I have a feeling that the mine, where ever it is, will hold the key."

"Perhaps," said Bob, "but more importantly, where would he bury the body. I suggest we begin our search right away. There are two camping shovels plus a Geiger counter in the jeep."

"Geiger counter?" asked Chano.

"Seems like the only way to find something that is buried. Bones are not easy without dogs to sniff them out, so I am counting on the body still having some metal, like a watch, or even teeth. Who knows?"

"Whew, you think of everything. OK, can I try the Geiger; never held one of these before?"

El Chano was instructed on how to use the counter, while Bob carried the shovels.

"Where do we start?" asked Chano, ready to turn it on.

"I would like to be as methodical as possible," said Bob. "Let's begin with a 20-foot radius around the shed. We can then expand on that if we have to." Bob paced it off and placed a couple of stakes at the 20-foot distance. They began, waiting for the Geiger to let them know there was something under foot.

A half hour later, they had completed the entire circumference, and all they had to show for it was a rusty old spur. Bob paced off another 20 feet, and away they went, with him now holding the machine.

"After all, that damn thing gets heavy," complained Chano.

All of a sudden the noise was loud and clear.

"Something close," said Bob, as he circled the area trying to zero in on the location.

"Right here!" he yelled excitedly. "Let's start digging; carefully now, we can pretend we are on a dig. They were only down about six inches when Bob was on his knees sifting the sand through his fingers. I've got something, but its not attached to a body. He took his handkerchief out, along with a plastic bag.

"It's a watch, and it has an inscription on the back. How lucky can we get?"

After wiping it clean Bob held it up to the sunlight. "It's a Rolex, and will you look at that. The name is Pete Stebbins. Hell, Chano, that's the guy who disappeared. There's no way he would leave an expensive trinket like this lying around on the desert. Wow, I love it when a hunch pays off."

They continued with the search until late afternoon when their stomachs put them in search of food. After all, it was a long time since the bacon. Neither one was of a mind to go hunting for dinner so they looked at the assortment of cans.

"Beans work for me," said Bob, "and there's a couple of hot dogs that we have to eat tonight. There's buns too, as well as the usual assortment of chips and pickles. We feast, my friend."

Two more beers mellowed the evening, and the dogs were beautifully roasted on a stick, as the beans heated themselves in the can.

"Desert?" teased Chano?

There was a can of peaches that they quickly devoured along with a couple of chocolate chip cookies that had started to melt. All in all, it was a successful and satisfying meal, and they wondered what they would do if they actually had to hunt for their food.

There were two hours of daylight left, so they decided to put it to good use and continue to search around the shack.

"Tomorrow we will find the mine, and maybe the claim, but that will be harder," mused Bob. "I just want to be sure we've done our due diligence here."

Due diligence was all that there was. That is, besides an old rusty tin cup, two spoons, and an old pocket watch, that, when cleaned and wound, actually worked.

That night, after watching the sun set once again, El Chano asked if Bob wanted the cot for the night. "I am sure I can manage the jeep, and you know, I slept like a baby on that old cot. Didn't wake up 'til I smelled your bacon cooking. I will never forget that glorious moment."

Bob threw a shoe at him, and proceeded to build up the fire for the night. "Need to look for more brush for tomorrow," he said. "The fire makes all the difference. Comforting, you know."

They said their good nights and settled into yet another night of peaceful desert sounds, as long as they were in the far distance, that is.

However, this night, they were not allowed to sleep undisturbed. Loud howling began about 2:15 and woke Chano first. He jumped out of the jeep and ran to stoke the fire, feeling that this was their first line of defense, however misguided.

Bob also was wakened and came outside to check. "Those sound like coyotes, not wolves, and they appear to be in distress. I wonder what could be so hungry he would want to take on a pack?"

"Mountain Lion would be my guess," said El Chano. Do you still have bullets for that 38 of yours:"

"Never fear, Davey Crockett is here,"

"He had a double barrel, I believe," said Chano, not a pea shooter."

"Hey, don't make fun of Ethel, here. She has seen me out of many a tough scrapes."

"Ethel?"

"Yep, Ethel. She was my first love; the gal I took to the junior prom. Wow, what a night. Vowed I would never forget her; ergo the pistol."

"I won't ask for any details; I do not believe any explaining is necessary. Hey, the coyotes are getting closer. Are they being chased?"

"That would be my guess. Let's get in the jeep and I'll turn the lights on. No, not for them; I want to see what I am shooting at."

They no sooner were peering out the windshield than two coyote passed the headlights about 15 feet away. Then there were three more.

"Will they attach?" asked Chano as he held on to the strap. And what about the top, is there time to put it up?"

"No time for that: get out the shells in the glove compartment, will you? This will repeat six times, but after that I have to reload. God, I hope my aim is on tonight. Start praying, there's two more."

And in answer to your question, any wild animal, if cornered, will attack to survive." There was a distinct groan from the passenger side.

"Bob, I counted 7; you have only six shots before you have to reload. Good grief. What do we do if the Mountain lion decides to join the party?"

"That's one hell of a guest list. Open the glove compartment and look under the Kleenex. Yeh, I've got another 38. Meet Henry. Know how to use one of those?"

"I know how to use one, but why the hell did you have to name him too? Or 'it,' see you've got me thinking like you."

"Henry was the best instructor at the academy; actually taught me how to shoot and never miss."

"OK, Henry, it is. Now where is the amo?"

"See those eyes over there to the left? Coyotes! Seems like they are taking some sort of refuge in our campsite. They must think the Mountain Lion may not come in this close. Good grief, they sure don't know the lion. Those beasts are cunning and patient. See the ring of darkness around us? You can bet the lion is just beyond that, ready and waiting."

"What are our options?" asked El Chano.

"Options? We just have to be more cunning."

"OK teach, how do we go about doing that?"

"All right, are you ready to have some fun? You cover the right side and I'll concentrate on our left. We can only hope they don't circle to the rear. Now, I am going to turn the lights off and count to 10, I don't think the coyotes will move, but I know the lion has a bead on every one of them. I want him to make a move. Shoot as soon as you see him; I'll do the same. Ready?"

El Chano thought that was the longest 10 seconds he ever lived through. Bob was right, when the lights came back on the lion was stealthy crossing their path heading for the coyote closest to the shack.

All hell broke out. Bob fired! Chano fired! The coyotes ran every which way; in fact one jumped over the hood of the jeep and almost got caught in the cross-fire. Then all was quiet. The coyotes were gone, but the mountain lion was still there.

Bob could see he was still alive, so he put his 38 to his head and fired. "What do you think, Chano, your first trophy for your newly decorated condo?"

"Trophy?" Chano laughed. "You want me to hang that head over my would-be fireplace?"

"What do you mean? He's a handsome fellow. If you don't want him we can drag him closer to the hills and he will be gone by noon."

"Any chance for sleep, or are we done for the night," asked Chano.

"Sleep? I hope so. I don't think anything is going to bother us for the next couple of hours. Sleep tight."

At first light, Bob and El Chano roped the lion and dragged him closer to the hills; they stocked the fire, and cracked a few eggs, followed by a complete surprise Bob had hidden under the seat of the jeep.

He held up the bag and announced, "I thought we would need a reward about now and hope they are not all dried out. Jelly Donuts, Chano. We earned 'em."

Later, with shovels in hand and their 38's loaded, they both started off toward the mushroom shape that they believed was near the suspect's mine.

The terrain was slow going because of all the smaller rocks that indicated a recent shaking of the earth. It was easy to see an avalanche had taken place as they looked toward the top of the hill and the now jagged side of the mushroom.

"Oh, no!" exclaimed El Chano. "See that dark spot up there, Bob, just at the base of the mushroom? I think that must be the entrance to the mine, but how the hell do we get there?"

"I guess we climb, Chano, but with these loose rocks, the going will be a bit treacherous. Let's start up over to the left; seems less hazardous there, but we'll see."

"I brought the lion rope" said Bob. You never know. Just be careful; test each step to be sure it isn't going to slide."

They found a clear area at the base and started to climb, but before long, the rocks started to set off more tumbling.

"Slower, slower!" yelled Bob. "We sure don't want to end up down there in a pile of bones."

El Chano reached an area of the mountain that was level with the mine. "Throw me your rope, Bob, I almost went down over there."

With the rope wrapped around Chano's shoulders and arms, Bob tied the other end around his waist, and began to climb. Chano eased the rope upward. Before long they were both level with the mine, and holding on to whatever they could grasp, they began inching sideways until they stood at the entrance. They walked inside.

The jeep really came prepared. Both unhooked their flashlight from their belt and flashed them around. Two black objects flew over their heads. "Bats!" yelled Chano. "I hate bats"

"Like I hate snakes," countered Bob. "The bats will leave us alone, Chano but watch out where you step. Rattlers like dark, cozy places, too."

They could see that the sides of the mine had been worked, so they turned a corner and were surprised at the open area they found.

"This large room must have been here for some time. That must be 20 feet in diameter. In fact, I think it was from the formation of these hills," said Bob. "I'm not a geologist, but by the looks of the stalactites, they have been holding on for a mighty long time."

El Chano laughed, "That brings me back. I remember, those from above hold 'tight' and those coming from the ground are stalagmites, pushing up with all their 'might.'

"Good job, you must have been an 'A' student."

"Most of the time, but don't ask me to draw an isosceles triangle."

"You mean the triangle with two sides of equal length?"

"Ha. Now who goes to the head of the class."

"Look at the ground in here. All sandy soil," said Chano,

"Easier to dig," said Bob. "The only problem is carrying him up here to bury."

"Not necessarily," argued Chano. "Seems like he would already be here working the mine when his partner bashed him over the head with a shovel, dug the grave, and voila, end of story."

"I like that scenario the best," said Bob. "I don't see any point using the Geiger anywhere else. I believe he is here, too."

"Since I like using the Geiger so much, would you mind if I came up here for a couple of hours, just to see what I can find?"

"Be my guest. I just wish our cell phones worked up here. We are totally incommunicado. However, that will give me time to work up my report tomorrow, always hoping that you are successful here in the mine. If so, we can even begin our trek back."

"Ha!" smiled El Chano. "I think you have had enough of prospecting, me amigo."

That afternoon, after checking the shed for any hidden nuggets, Bob decided that it might be fun to have some fresh meat for dinner. "Hay, Chano, I'm going hunting. Any requests?"

"Based on what I know to be in the butchers showcase, the only choices are coyote, mountain lion, and rattlers. I have not seen one jack rabbit, or prairie dog, (alive, that is), even though I have seen their holes. I guess whatever you manage to snare, we could possibly eat. My contribution will be to find two sticks to hold our dinner over the fire."

It was 4:00 PM, and El Chano had not heard a word or gun shot. He was beginning to worry. After all, where there was one mountain lion, there was bound to be others.

Then, finally at 5:05, there was a gunshot. One single shot, and Chano felt that Bob hit his mark. If truth be told, he was not at all excited, and was kind of looking forward to that can of spam fried on the skillet.

Just minutes later Bob came into view carrying a stick with something wrapped around it and slung over his shoulder.

"Oh no!" cried Chano. "Bob, you know I hate rattle snakes."

"Tastes just like chicken, Chano, you'll see."

Chapter 15

Survival

Actually, the rattlesnake did taste a little like chicken, but they ended up opening the spam, anyway. That night, Bob was back in the shack, mostly because of his hectic day of hunting. El Chano stoked the fire and prepared for a peaceful night in the jeep. The sky was clear, the moon was bright, the air, a little crisp, but perfect for that much needed night's sleep.

Yes, they both slept like babies, probably because they believed that the next day would see their mission accomplished, and the jeep turned around and headed home. Such a wonderful dream.

Following some flapjacks, which proved to be the most satisfactory thing they managed to cook thus far, El Chano was excited to try the Geiger on the mine. "Take the rope with you," urged Bob, and be sure your gun is loaded." Meet you back here by 11:00. That would be plenty of time to get to the ranch."

El Chano nodded, waved and took off for the mushroom hill.

"I'll have everything packed and ready to go," yelled Bob, as El Chano marched away.

"First things first," said Bob as he checked the water supply and saw that they still had half a plastic container. Then he filled the other three canteens, two for each of them in case they had to trapse far from home base. After that Bob busied himself packing their belongings, and digging a hole for the garbage they had created.

Then, because of the big day yesterday, he felt that a nice nap would do him a world of good before he traversed the jeep back to civilization. He stepped inside the shack and stretched out on the cot. He slept.

He was not sure what woke him, just that the sound of metal on metal was something he was not expecting to hear.

"Could Chano be back already?" he asked himself, as he drew his 38 and tiptoed to the door. Then he saw it. Someone was actually fooling around with the jeep.

"Hey!" he cried. "What the hell do you think you are doing?"

He ran outside with his pistol drawn. Then he heard the motor on the other side of the jeep, and the next thing he knew a man with helmet and visor, revved his motorcycle, and road away in a cloud of dust.

Bob ran for the jeep. It wouldn't start. Now he knew what the so and so was doing. He jumped from the vehicle and ran after him on foot. No use, so he stopped, aimed and fired three rounds before he realized he was too far away.

"I really believe I hit the bastard," he growled under his breath. "I have to find out," he vowed, so he took off again on foot. There, at the point where the motorcycle disappeared over the rise, was a trail of blood. A much more exuberant Lieutenant began running back to camp.

He stepped in a rabbit hole, fell to the ground, and let out a yelp that echoed around the canyon.

"Oh, dear God, I broke it."

There is no question that the shots and even the yelp were heard up at the mine. Chano had just had a loud Geiger response and started digging. He hit something soft and found it was a leg. Then he cleared away an arm and hand. On the hand was a very large ring, and wondered why the killer did not remove this obviously expensive diamond.

"Well," thought El Chano, this bobble is what set off the Geiger. Now, to cover him up and see what the hell Bob is yelling about.

Before he reached the shack, there was Bob, holding his leg, and sitting on the desert floor. He hurried over.

One look told him that it was broken, so he offered to run and get the jeep.

"The jeep won't run. It was skuttled, and so are we. I believe our killer was here checking on us, hoping to eliminate us from the game. We are in a real fix, Chano. The only water we have left is that which we have in our canteens. Hell!"

"When did you fill the canteens?"

"Just before he shuttled us. But now that we have no vehicle, we are going to have to walk out of this God forsaken place. Hell!"

"The only good thing is that I managed to hit him before he escaped. Hell! He escaped."

"OK, first things first. Let's get you back to the shack. Can you stand?"

Slowly the process began, and Bob managed to stand on one foot, the pain from the broken ankle shooting up his leg.

"Hold on to me, Bob, and let's start hopping. Let's not even think of the alternative." It took a while, but in about 30 minutes they stood by the jeep inspecting the damage.

"Hell is right," yelled Chano. He punctured the gas line as well as slashed the plastic water container. We are up a creek, Bob. Now, let's be calm and figure this out. Come on, buddy, we can make it."

It took a few minutes for Chano to wrap his ankle with bandages from the first aid kit supported by twigs for some stability. Bob was still barely able to stand.

"There's only one solution, Bob. I will make you comfortable, and begin my walk back to that ranch. If we both sit here and do nothing, we are toast, literally."

Bob looked over at El Chano, his jaw resolutely set. He was as serious as anyone could be under the circumstances.

"Yes," agreed Bob, under one condition; you take two canteens and leave me the smaller one. We will share what is left of our provisions, with you taking the larger portion because you have to keep up your energy."

El Chano looked over at Bob. "Deal," he said. "Now, I am going to fix a lean-to here so you can have some shelter, and still see what is going on. No more ambushes."

Chano moved the cot right by the door, and positioned the blanket overhead like a canopy to shield him from the afternoon sun. I know it has holes, but it will work for the most part. You can't stay in the shed, it will roast you alive this afternoon. Now, let's divide the spoils. They shared the two cans of spam which they both felt was the best meal of the bunch. There were some cookies, a couple of rolls, and 3 hard boiled eggs, and two cans of beans which Chano opened so they could eat those first.

They divided the shells, and before they knew it, El Chano waved a good by, and with a pack over his back, headed to what he believed was the opening to the canyon.

"Hell," he said.

Bob wanted to doze, but couldn't. How can you get your mind to stop. All he could think of was Chano and that hot sun beating on his back. The only thing that cheered him was the fact that Chano said he had hit pay dirt. "The body was there." Bob waited to eat his beans, and when he figured it was close to sunset he dipped in his spoon.

"It's called survival," he whispered to himself.

As the moon shown right overhead, all Bob could think about was El Chano; was he sleeping tonight, or did he keep on walking? They both knew that everything looks different at night and it is so easy to lose your way.

"Not Chano," thought Bob. He will always keep the mountain to his back. The moon will always show the silhouette."

To this day he doesn't know how he managed to sleep, but he did, and while you sleep you don't drink. By morning there was still half a canteen left.

He managed to get a raw egg down along with a cookie. "Breakfast enough," he said to himself.

They were approaching the hottest part of the day, and he decided to nibble on a roll, which, of course made him want to drink. If Bob had heard the news report, he would have shuddered. They predicted 110 degrees at 4:00 PM. It was better he didn't know.

Nothing stirred, nothing flew! The little desert canyon was as quiet as a ghost. Not even the coyote thought howling would do any good. Bob tried not to drink that night, but the effects of the heat was taking it's toll.

By morning, in between fitful tossing, he may have slept some, but he was totally exhausted and his ankle was throbbing relentlessly. He started to become delirious and reached over for his canteen and drank. It was now empty.

The temperature was to increase to 115. Again, it wouldn't have helped Bob to know.

He was thirsty, he was hungry. He looked at what was left of his stash. He wondered what the spam would do. There was some liquid there. He had barely enough strength to open the can and began to sip on the tasty droppings around the meat. He was afraid to eat, so he leaned back and thought of El Chano. Where could he be. Then he wondered where he really was. His leg was paining so much that he couldn't tell any more why it was hurting. He remembered his ski accident years ago, and thought that must be it. The sun continued to beat. There is no doubt that by 5:00 he was dehydrated

He looked up through the blanket that Chano used for his canopy. He smiled. How pretty that is with all those sparkly beams coming through. Then he was alerted.

A noise, louder than anything he had ever heard, was coming at him. "This must be it," he thought. "It must be my time to go." He looked through the hole in the canopy and saw what looked like arms getting closer and closer, louder and louder.

"Bob, Bob, it seemed to say.

"Yes, I am here. Come and get me."

"Bob, it's Chano. We are going to make it. I've got the biggest, blackest helicopter you ever saw."

Chapter 16

The Crutch of the Matter

"I have always hated these things, even when other people use them," commented Bob, as he hobbled out the door of the Emergency room with El Chano at his elbow.

Woops! The automatic doors closed quickly and caught one of Bob's crutches. The expletives poured forth, but between El Chano and him, they managed to escape the hungry jaws.

Crossing the parking lot was Bob's first opportunity to master the metal monsters. He reached the car and when he looked at the space that he was going to have to navigate his cast, he began to have misgivings.

"Chano, do you think I can drive this thing?"

"I would bring the seat back as far as I can, then try to get in and see how much room you have left. If it doesn't work, you can always commandeer Luis to be your driver. I am sure he will be more than thrilled."

Bob grimaced as he pushed the lever and moved the seat back. "It only gave me 2 inches at most. I already had it opened up; I have pretty long legs."

He got his right side and leg in OK, but lifting that heavy cast was another matter. It took both hands to lift his leg in, and only then, did he give a great sigh of relief.

El Chano placed the crutches in the back seat and waved him on to the road. "No freeway today," he smiled to himself.

Bob was happy to finally drive into the underground parking of his condo; and doubly pleased to find his usual parking place waiting for him. Now to exit. He knew he would only have the cast for a short time before graduating into a boot, but now was now, and lifting the leg out of the car was still a chore. Once out he opened the back to retrieve the crutches. That's when it happened, almost on cue.

Two shots rang out. Almost instinctively he raised his crutch, and both bullets were miraculously deflected. He dropped the metal arms, grabbed his 38 with his right hand and his phone with the left. He fired one round just to let his assailant know he was armed and alive.

"Officer in trouble!" he screamed into the phone. This is Lieutenant Mendoza, bring the army, sirens blaring." He barely got out the address when he heard the first welcome siren getting closer and closer. Two more shots bounced off the hood, and then there was silence.

Three, four, then five cars, all flashing their lights and singing, rolled into the garage. What a sight. Out jumped Luis and crouched down beside him.

"You OK, boss? Where is he?"

"Never saw him. The shots came from over there, near the exit sign. My guess would be that he is now long gone."

"You stay put, boss; I'll join the rest and help with the search. Stay safe," he said as he glanced over at the crutches. "Did you know you have two bullet punctures in those things?"

"Yep, probably saved my life."

Suddenly quiet settled over the garage and Bob breathed a full breath of air. Then he heard a familiar voice coming from the elevator and he smiled. All the troubles and pain of the past few days just melted away. He stood up and waved. It was Stella.

When she saw his head pop up over the hood of the car, she smiled the warmest smile that literally warmed him to the bone. Then she started running. He tried to stop her, fearful that the assailant might still be lurking around, but she kept coming.

Leaning on the car, he hobbled around to meet her. Then, before either one knew what was happening, they were holding tightly to one another. He looked into her face and saw the tears.

Neither one could speak, so they kept holding on to each other, almost afraid to separate, for fear the magic would disappear. It didn't.

"You have no idea," she cried, "when I called your office, they told me you were rescued by helicopter from the desert. Are you really all-right?"

He bent over and kissed her as firmly and assuredly as he could. "I am OK now; the moment I heard your voice, it was like all the dark clouds vanished. Let me grab my crutches and let's get inside. I am starved. Do you have any food?"

She actually burst out laughing. "For you, my love, I always have food."

Once upstairs he collapsed on the sectional; a little slower, now, because of the weight at the end of his left leg. But for now, the leg didn't seem to matter. He was here, Stella was here, and he was going to eat. Anything would be an improvement over those bars they gave him on the helicopter; somebody said they were protein, but he questioned their relationship to any food group.

He could still hear the roaring sound that he first heard on the desert. He thought it was his ride to heaven; well, in a way it was. This was heaven to him, and Stella, the most beautiful angel he had ever seen."

It only took 20 minutes to put together an omelet with an English muffin; and she remembered, lots of marmalade on the side. However, when she walked back into the living room, the head of the homicide department was still seeing and hearing the helicopter. He was fast asleep.

Meanwhile at County, El Chano sat across from his brother, Antonio, once again. After a couple of days in jail his attitude had changed considerably, but he was still very much on the defensive.

"I hope you have interrogated that irritating Sylvia person who made such a ruckus the night of the murder. Seems to me," continued Antonio, "that someone that is capable of making so much noise about nothing is worth considering. And now that Clare is gone, as well as her manager, Juan, I have a little bit of gossip to tell."

"No tall tails, now Antonio. I know how you like to embellish and how, as a boy, you protected yourself at all cost."

"Ah, si. However, this is not one of those times. You see Sylvia was the real hustler. She was going with Juan at the time of his death. Can't prove it, but they are said to have had a fight to end all fights and he vowed never to lay eyes on that bimbo, ever again. Of course, she was furious, and you know the saying about a woman scorned etc.."

"OK," said El Chano, "you know how easily Bob can tear a story apart if somebody lies. I would be carful, if I were you."

"No worries, brother, but there is more. All the people at that table that night had their secrets. All, except, thee and thou, and of course Rosa."

El Chano held up his hand, "Unless you want to stay here forever waiting for your execution, you better tell it straight."

"You are trying to scare me, and believe me, I am already scared clear through. This time it is about Manuel. Everybody loves the guy. He always appears so easy-going, and easy-to-know. That is until somebody crosses him. I have never seen a guy change so fast. Even his face gets all deranged, and his voice takes on a deeper, louder tone. Scary, if you ask me. He is worth checking into for sure, even though I don't have anything specific to pin on him." Antonio sat back, clearly pleased with himself.

El Chano's eyes narrowed, "You know, brother, I'll do anything to help you, but you've got to play it straight with me or I'll abandon you in an instant."

"You wouldn't dare. You promised mom you would look after me, and a promise is a promise. Both Rosa and I are counting on you. She was in yesterday and said she was depending on you."

A very distinct groan came from El Chano before he slide back his chair and left the interrogation room.

"Why does life have to be so damn complicated. Now I guess I will really have to get to work, with or without Bob's crutched assistance."

Instead of going back to his hotel he decided to stop and see how the invalid was doing. Actually, the timing couldn't be more perfect. Bob had just woken up from his nap, completely embarrassed, so he decided to depart for his own condo. After all, omelets do not preserve well, and neither do grumpy Lieutenants.

He had just opened a beer and settled down, deciding that a brew was preferrable to any more meds until bedtime, when the doorbell rang.

He was now hobbling on one crutch, so he made the door in record time and was pleased to see El Chano. "Brew time," he announced, and pointed Chano to the fridge. "And another for me, too, if you don't mind."

Each man relaxed, wondering where to begin their individual tale, especially after the time they spent together, that some may refer to as bonding, but no one we know would ever go down that path.

Finally, El Chano cleared his throat and began. "Got some information for you, well little more than gossip, but I wanted to share and see if you had followed up on either Manuel or Sylvia."

"Ah Sylvia; the accuser at the table the night of the murder. She was interrogated by Luis, and he concluded that she was overly jealous of Clare. Then, when we discovered Clare was murdered, we looked more closely at Sylvia. Bad reputation. I think she played around with everyone at that celebrity table. I couldn't figure out how she fit in. I guess she was always somebody's flavor of the month."

"If it is true that one guy killed himself over her, or Clare, and others were obsessed by her charms, seems like a recipe for disaster."

"Got an idea," beamed Bob. Since you want to get your badge," he laughed, "how about checking out the lovely Sylvia, yourself. A Margareta or two may do the trick."

El Chano smiled. "So you think I can charm the truth out of her? I can give it a shot. I can always use the line that I promised my dear sainted mother that I would watch over my baby brother; and now he is almost on death row. That sob story should sell. The problem is it is no sob-story, and Antonio reminded me of my promise earlier today."

"Good man," said Bob, as he raised his glass to salute his friend. "You take on Sylvia and I'll tackle Manuel. Between us we'll solve this case. Have to; and when this is over," he raised his cast," I have a cruise to take, that is after you act as my best man,"

Both men raised their glasses, and Chano actually let out a yahoo!!!!

"One more question, are there any leads on the motorcycle desert thief?"

"Too damn slippery. The state police are trying to help trace his escape. Where the hell did he disappear to. There has to be something south of where we were. Just because we don't know about it doesn't mean it doesn't exist. Say, would you be game to another trip out there to see if we can solve that one?"

There was a loose pillow on the couch that became air-borne and almost spilled Bob's beer. "You know what you can do with that idea," chuckled Chano as he headed toward the door. "I think I'll give Sydney a call. Maybe she is free tonight."

Chapter 17

Undercover

Once El Chano arrived in his hotel room, he just stood there and looked around, lamenting the fact that this was not his home; there was nothing here that belonged to him that gave him the comfort he was looking for right now. He shook his head. The contractor told him personally that it would be another month or two before his condo would be ready for occupancy, and another two after that before the areas that were burned would be fully restored.

"Time," he said to himself, "such an enigma. The only thing I can do is to concentrate on the task at hand and solve this damn mystery, and get brother Antonio out of prison." He laughed, "In that order of course; it wouldn't hurt him to have time to think about the rest of his life and to realize how close he came to a life in prison, or worse."

He reached in his pocket and pulled out his pad where he had scribbled Sylvia's number that Bob had given him. He stared at it for a minute then dialed, a bitter-sweet taste now lingering in his mouth.

"I'm a damn spy," he announced to himself, when the slow, smooth voice of Sylvia answered the phone. His voice almost stuck in his throat, but he finally found it.

"Sylvia, this is El Chano, I have been thinking about you and was wondering if you were too busy to join me for dinner tonight . We had a fire and I am presently a displaced person."

"No, displaced, not misplaced," she almost gushed, and agreed to meet him at Luige's at 7:00.

"Whew," he breathed, "now, how the hell am I going to pull this off? Intrigue has never been my strong suit, and I am going to have to rehearse my interrogation technique. He poured a beer, grabbed his pad, and began making a list of questions he hoped he would be able to ask with an air of innocence.

"First, I will have to review that suicide case, and why she felt that Clare was responsible, even indirectly. Of course, she is the perfect one to ask about all the other men seated at the celebrity table the night of Clare's murder. He turned the page and drew a picture of the table. He knew Clare always sat at the end so she could run off and prepare for her performance. On her left, was poor Juan, her manager, who they found skewered in the freezer. Then, at the other end of the table was Manuel, who, according to Antonio, was a mystery man. And next to him sat his daughter, Gladys, a slight, very beautiful woman. That leaves Don Diego at the head of the table with Sylvia on his left followed by my illustrious family."

"Seems like that will take the whole evening," he smiled , "I only hope she is one of those, who, once they start talking will never stop until she gets to the end. I would love to have a tape recorder in my pocket, but they have now made that illegal.

"I had better start getting ready; this is one assignment I don't want to mess up."

On the other side of town, in a cluster of duplexes surrounding a parklike setting, Sylvia was throwing dress after dress on her bed. Once it was totally covered, she studied her choices; everything from black to a large hibiscus floral, reminiscent of Hawaii. The decision made; she gathered up all but one, leaving the black, v-neck, that followed the curves of her body, that she painstakingly worked so hard to maintain.

The steamy fragrance floated out the bathroom door as she showered, and, later, it actually took her twenty minutes to get every hair in place and her makeup flawless. She stood in front of the mirror pleased with her efforts, even though her mind often questioned why El Chano sought her out at this particular time.

"Hmmm, is he really interested in me or is this some kind of a ploy to get information that he will pop back to the Lieutenant? Either way" she thought, "I'll get a great meal, and who knows, maybe even a good time."

Two browned legs with leopard pumps stepped out of the taxi, stood for a moment in front of Luigi's, then headed for the double, etched-glass doors. Once inside El Chano was at her elbow and escorted her to his always reserved, romantic table behind the palms. It seems he had these tables all over town. It didn't matter, because she was enchanted, and even chuckled coquettishly.

El Chano hadn't noticed before, but now, as every head turned, Sylvia was a damn attractive woman. True the blond hair wasn't natural, but who cares. And those flirty eyelashes, and voluptuous lips and endowments were not to be taken lightly. She was a babe and he was not surprised that she held court with every man at the celebrity table, probably more.

Our charming Sylvia also noticed the suave, masculine stature of her escort as he glided her across the dining room to their romantic alcove. He was tall, well, tall enough; he was handsome, and he had eyes that could literally melt any heart as well as the jewels off the richest debutant, if there were any in the room.

"Champagne?" he asked, his voice just a few notes above sultry. However, if you were to ask El Chano how

157

down- right sexy he was coming across to his escort he would probably deny it. He would be wrong.

The champagne was ordered, as was the dinner. El Chano always left that to the chef, and knew it would be the best the house had to offer.

As he reached for the bottle to pour some more champagne, their hands touched. He was surprised he felt the same attraction that many men before him had experienced. It was intoxicating,

It is also widely known that when that happens, the woman is also aware that she has made a new conquest, and is definitely encouraged in her flirtatiousness. El Chano was an easy target, responding in kind with his own sexual innuendoes. Their knees brushed, their hands often met across the table, and at one point he even got up, walked behind her chair, and planted two caressing kisses on her neck. Dinner arrived.

They were both caught in the moment and hardly noticed the excellent shrimp and linguini that sat before them. However, duty did call and each did justice to the chef's cuisine.

How it happened, nobody knows, but all of a sudden, Sylvia asked El Chano how the investigation was going.

"Ah, finally," he whispered to himself. "An opening."

"There is just one point I am curious about and that is why you feel the late Clare was in any way responsible for Alberto's suicide."

"I meant what I said that night," she replied, "of course, I didn't know she was dead. I think I knew her better than most. When I first came to town she asked me to share her apartment with her. I had my own room, and the rent was reasonable. We did this for about eight months, but she had quite a revolving door. At that time I was more interested in making a living, and when I came home at night I was ready to crash."

"What exactly was this revolving door? She just had a lot of boy friends, or what?"

"Or what, would be more to the point. When she first started going with Alberto; his full name was Alberto Sanchez. He was nice; not as handsome as you," she gushed, "but an all- around good guy."

"I happened to be home and shared some champagne with them one night. It was easy to see what she was after. Once she learned he had a gold mine her eyes lit up. It was quite an experience for me too, and not long after that I left. I got to know him, because I was often in the apartment before she came home. We became friends, and I thought he would ask me out at one point, but Clare was quite a charmer. He never knew what hit him."

"But suicide," continued El Chano, "that's a big accusation."

"Not really. He was having trouble making ends meet and depended on that gold mine. Humph, he was finagled out of it hook, line and sinker. I don't know for sure if he lost it at cards, but I always felt Clare had something to do with it. Oh, maybe not by herself, but I had a sense that there was someone in the shadows, maybe even a mastermind that called all the shots. Sure looked awful fishy to me. Say, is there any more champagne in that bottle?"

"We'll get another," announced El Chano, and signaled the waiter.

Later that night El Chano dropped by Bob's condo hoping he would still be up. He was, and only because Bob had slept for hours already, was he anxious to get El Chano's report.

"Lay it on me Chano. Was it worth it?"

"Got any beer, had much too much champagne to keep up with that gal. Beer first," and he headed for the fridge. Once relaxed on the couch he breathed deeply and began.

"She was really something, Bob. I mean, really something. I think I was the envy of the restaurant. She had the looks, the moves; you name it, it was there, all packaged in the best there was. Wow!"

"OK, I can see it." said Bob, "now what the hell did you learn?

"What would you say if I said the word 'gold?'"

"You mean like in 'gold mine?'"

"Yep, exactly that. Bob, I think we finally have a connection. This one is up to your office and all their great facilities and electronics. I can smell it, Bob, I really can, and I think this is going to make full circle to our favorite candidate. The only one I didn't get around to was Manuel. Sylvia sat across from him at the celebrity table and Gladys sat next to him. Who is Gladys?"

Bob smiled, "Finally, a question I can answer. Gladys is Manuel's daughter. She is only 18, and some believe she is also the daughter of Clare. We are checking on that one, too. Pretty hard but we did find that the young Gladys was married for a few months to a man by the name of Stebbins. Hey! wait a minute he yelled, as he reached for the folder at his elbow. Yes, here it is. They identified the corpse you discovered in the mine as Stebbins, Pete Stebbins. And guess who the mine was registered to? It was Stebbins and what's-his-name: the guy that Stella said killed himself, the night of the first murder. Wow!"

"OK, OK, said El Chano, as he pulled out his notebook. I have to get all these names straight in my mind."

"First we have the suicide guy, Alberto Sanchez, who just happened to have a gold mine. I would be anxious to know if it is the same one where we found poor Pete Stebbens. Holy socks, Bob, this plot is thickening. Proverbial pea soup, if you ask me. I am thinking that Alberto and Pete knew each other. Pete was killed and buried, and now, Alberto had to die, maybe because he knew something."

"Good figuring," said Bob, and I'm going to call in our suspicions right now," and he grabbed his cell.

El Chano listened as he went over to the refrigerator and got two more beers. He hardly got seated again when the phone rang.

Bob smiled before he hung up. "Bingo! You got it right on the money, Chano. In fact, Alberto and Peter were actually partners in a mine, and it was recorded that black nuggets were turned in that totaled over 5 pounds."

"Whew!" exclaimed Chano, "talk about a formula for murder. What do you think, Bob, is this a Domino effect?"

"I think so; my only concern is whether or not the last Domino has fallen."

Chapter 18

Dominoes, Anyone?

Bob lay awake that night thinking about the case and trying to compare it to any other he had ever had. He was clue and motive hunting. Well, not really motive; it had to be greed; gold fever.

He must have fallen asleep because it was almost three o'clock when he sat bolt up-right in bed. "Re-enactment!, of the night of the murder, with a twist. Of course, just like in Martha Millers locked room mystery, the Three of Spades. Only this time it will be dominos on the table instead of cards."

He picked up the phone and dialed Luis and told him that tomorrow afternoon they were going to gather all the survivors that sat at the celebrity table at the time of the murders. "We are going to play Dominoes, Luis. Just be sure they are all there. I will fill you in tomorrow over a jelly donut."

On the way to the station, Bob maneuvered his leg out the SUV and into the donut shop. Then he walked two doors down to a game shop and picked up the largest

Domino game he had ever seen. He smiled in anticipation, maneuvered his leg back into the SUV and headed downtown.

When he arrived at the station, Luis was actually pacing back and forth around their desks, a worried expression etched on his face.

Luis ran to get the coffees as Bob opened the bag of donuts. "OK, tell me what has got you in a dither"

"Boss, do you have any idea what day this is?"

"Day?" asked Bob. "It's Tuesday," he replied, and when he said it, a light bulb went on in his head. "No, you're kidding. You don't think?"

"All I know, Bob, is that people have been dying on Taco Tuesday much too often. And today is another Taco Tuesday."

"My word, Luis, if we count the bodies, just here in California, we have four to date, and that includes the one found in the mine as well as the suicide.

They both sat down at their desks and contemplated their donut. Luis looked up. "Bob, you don't think this guy would go for number five?"

"Well, we know he has gone for more than that if we count Nevada. But for my book, we are dealing with a class 'A' narcissus that believes he can get away with anything he can think of. Look at his record to date. Luis, we have to be more prepared today than we ever have before. The only good thing is that he doesn't have enough time to plan or prepare one of his extravaganzas. There is comfort in that. Let's enjoy our donuts."

"There is just one thing boss, both murders at the restaurant were on Taco Tuesday. Do you think we should wait until tomorrow?"

"Hell, no. We would only be giving him more time to prepare."

Needless to say, Bob's avant-garde demeanor was just slightly exaggerated. He had come to respect the cunning of this adversary, as well as his intellectual prowess. He had to admit to himself that he was on edge, but vowed that the restaurant be well protected, and the participants in his little game be in no danger. Well, with the exception of one, if that was even a remote possibility. But yes, he did remember that Clare died on Taco Tuesday, as did Juan. No, he didn't think it was coincidental, and yes, he wouldn't put it past the killer to try for another murder if there was motive or opportunity. And Bob, for one, was not going to let him out of his sight; that is if he really knew who the killer was.

"Good grief," he thought, "was he really starting to second guess himself?"

Bob had given instructions for officers to be placed at all exits and in the hall to the lavatories. "No repeat performances," he mumbled as he set out the dominos on the table.

Luis walked up and looked at the display. "Boss, am I supposed to figure out that crazy pattern of yours? And look at the size of those dominos. They look like a kid's toy."

"Maybe so, but somebody at the table will figure it out. We will have to watch these three names carefully," he said, as he passed the list along to Luis. One of them is the worst kind of killer there is. One, without a soul. Now, just let me test this one time, so I know it will work."

He nudged the Domino on the upper right and they started to fall, even the arm, which was tricky,

Luis's eyes grew big with understanding, "I got it boss, pretty clever. Oh, oh, set 'em up, here come the players."

"Damn, Taco Tuesday," said Luis, out loud. "I'll never think of it in the same way again," he whispered to Bob, as they ushered in the Domino spectators.

Antonio was let out of prison on bail, and was accompanied by El Chano and his sister Rosa. Sylvia sat on the other side of Antonio following the place cards that indicated the same seats they had at the last gathering. Don Diego, the manager, took his place at the head of the table, leaving only two more chairs occupied; Manuel and Gladys. The two chairs representing Juan and Clare were

166

leaning with their backs on the table, a graphic reminder of their fate.

Drink orders were taken, and a light lunch would be served following Bob's demonstration. But for the present, there was an air of anticipation. No one spoke, but simply sat quietly, each one looking at the other, almost accusatorily. They couldn't help but see the unusual Domino display, and Bob knew only one would be able to figure it out. Then the show began without any fan-fare or drum-roll.

Bob had been sitting at the foot of the table, but now stood and addressed his audience.

"I thank you all for coming. I thought it was important to bring you up to date on the investigation since each of you was a witness in his or her own way."

"That first Taco Tuesday, several weeks ago now, was an event we will all remember. The killer made sure of that. Not only was poor Clare killed in a bazaar way in the lavatory, but there were also sideshows. There was the scream that startled everyone, and many of you started running for the door or slid under the table."

"Ah, then there were the snakes; an event carefully planned to create chaos for a very distinct purpose. Then, one of the snakes slithered over to Rosa, and bit her leg, right . . . ."

Everyone turned, but Rosa was gone.

"Where the hell is she?" yelled Bob.

Then it happened again. The scream ripped across the room, and El Chano jumped up and headed for the lavatories. "She just said powder-room and left," he called over his shoulder.

Bob was right behind him. "Luis, you stay and keep your eye on everyone."

Once out of sight, they stopped in the hall, and had all they could do to keep from laughing. El Chano shook his head as Rosa joined them.

"Seemed real to me," said Rosa. "Just like last time. When can I go back in?"

"After I begin my Domino talk. I want someone in there to get a little rattled. I know that's asking for a lot, but we've got to start punching back. I don't want another murder. OK, I'm going in. Chano, bring her back in a couple."

Bob walked over to his seat and assured everyone that she would be alright. I would like all of you to look at the Dominos. These represent the case as it stands now, and I don't want to add any more dominos. Why?" He reached over and flicked the one at top and they began to fall.

"Each one of those represents a death. Actually, a brutal murder committed by someone so determined to get to his end game that he will stop at nothing."

"But there are six dominos and we only have had two murders, unless you are including Alberto's suicide?" questioned Sylvia."

"Yes, we are including Alberto. That investigation has been reopened, and we have reason to believe it was murder."

"I knew it!" shouted Sylvia. "I just couldn't see him shooting himself. I was right!"

"Yes, you were right, and our department offers our collective apologies for not investigating further. But now, with all the additional evidence from the other murders, it gives us a case to go forward with."

Everyone stood to look at the Dominos. "That accounts for three of them," remarked Manuel. "Do we know about the others?"

Bob continued, "Information led us to the desert outside Palm Springs to look for clues. You see, there was gold involved. We discovered that Alberto Sanchez owned part of a mine. We had a map of sorts and followed it to yet, another body. This body was buried inside the gold mine, itself. Forensics tells us that the time of death was after that of Alberto. The person in the mine was Pete Stebbens, who, we understand, had initially found the mine and went in with Alberto to begin mining."

"Now we are up to four bodies, all, we believe, because of Gold Fever. The two dominos at the top resent murders that took place in Nevada during a mining exhibition from UNLV."

"Is there a connection? Yes, we believe so, and the Nevada police are working with us to prove just that."

Ladies and gentlemen, the main reason I am presenting all this to you is for your own health and well-being. Two of your own have been killed, and we believe that at least one of you may know something that could be harmful to you. We are up against a ruthless killer. He will stop at nothing. I urge you, if you have any information, or just a gut feeling, please let us know."

"This killer has a flair for the dramatic and bazaar, and I don't want to be called in some Taco Tuesday just to discover your body hanging from that rafter up there."

Everyone looked up and shuddered. Bob's speech had its effect. The waiters started arriving with the food, but right now the patrons were a solum group, each one deep in his own thoughts with fear etched on their faces.

The salmon was pushed around the plates, with some actually ending up in the tacos. Margareta's were replenished more than once, but conversation was at an all-time low. Eyes were darting left and right, questioning and full of suspicion, but no one came up to either Bob or Luis and asked for an interview.

Almost on cue, one by one, they stood up and exited the restaurant. In Bob's mind it was anti-climactic. He was sure someone knew something, but Bob also knew human nature, and most folks believed they could outsmart even the cleverest killer. He shook his head. "Damn, this isn't going to end well."

Later that afternoon Bob entered the doctor's office anxious to be relieved of his cast. He felt sure his disposition would change once he was freed from the weight and graduated to a light boot.

The doctor looked at him, "You look stressed. Is the cast giving you trouble or is your job bringing you down."

"Both, actually, but mostly the job. Why do people insist on keeping secrets that could potentially kill them?"

"The human species," said the doctor, "is very much full of himself and his own ability to do the impossible. Sometimes it serves him well, but other times . . . ."

"Other times," continued Bob, "it gets them killed. I can't save 'em, Doc. I could lock them up, but they would hire a lawyer and be out in an instant. Now I guess I just sit by and wait for the call. This job is getting me down. I was hoping the boot would help my disposition. Don't think so." And he heard the last piece of plaster cast hit the floor. "Feels a hell of a lot better, though,"

He stepped inside the boot and walked around the room. "Is this the only color?"

"Yes, they say black goes with everything," laughed the Doc.

"Just be careful. Go about your business, but try not to put too much weight on it for another week. OK, get out of here. Take your girl out tonight and celebrate."

"Celebrate the up and coming murder of this madman's next victim?"

"Get out of here!" yelled Doc, and almost threw the plaster at him.

He picked up his cell and called El Chano. "Hey buddy, are you using your lair at Lugi's?"

El Chano laughed and said he would call and tell them you would be inhabiting, Good luck, buddy."

After calling Stella, he hurried home to shower and change. "Yes, the Doc was right, this was exactly the ticket," However, by the time he stepped into his grey slacks, he began to falter, still uneasy about the possibility of another murder.

"There must be something we can do to solve this thing. Something,"

By the time he stepped out of the elevator he knew what had to be done. He felt better. "Solutions tomorrow! Stella, tonight!"

Chapter 19

More Prospecting

"No, you're not!" said Stella, feeling emboldened after two glasses of champagne. "Look, you just got your cast off, and are recovering from your last adventure. How can you possibly think of returning to that horrible place. He almost killed you."

"I know, Stella. I don't want to go either, but there is unfinished business there. Remember, the killer rode into camp, cut our fuel lines, slashed our water jug and took off. Well, where did he take off to? The State Police couldn't find where he disappeared to, but maybe we can. My guess is that the old prospector had a place somewhere in those hills. It has to be there, Stella, and I am hoping there is evidence there, enough to prevent another murder.'

"When are you going?"

"Tomorrow, but first I want to do a helicopter search. I have a hunch."

"All right, then, but we celebrate tonight. After all, it has been over two weeks since you asked me to marry you. Is it time for a repeat performance?"

Bob's face was notably pinker, and he was pounding with happiness. He smiled. "Stella, let me finish this case and I promise you will get the finest, most elaborate proposal you have ever had. By the way, how many have you had?"

She clapped her hands, stood up, ran around the table, and planted a very firm kiss; a very long kiss; dead center.

They both agreed that an early night was the best for the situation at hand.

"Bob, you know I want you in my bed, but I also want you alive. A good night's rest will probably assure that more than a romp. Right?"

He stepped forward and held her close. "Stell, you really are the greatest. Remind me to tell you at least once a day for the rest of our lives."

They said good night, and he went back to his condo to begin preparations. Helicopter first, then El Chano. He secured them both, as well as Luis who was 'hell bent' to go.

"And Chano, double the supply of water. We are going to hide one someplace known only to us and the sidewinders"

The sun was high in the sky before El Chano and Luis turned their jeep between the rocks that were now all too familiar to Chano.

Luis was drinking it all in, and feeling secure that they had provided for every contingency. "It's this damn heat," he said. "Now I can better understand Bob's experience. It must have been hell. Yours too, Chano, walking out with hardly any water."

Suddenly the giant roar loomed above them, and the famous black helicopter flew over with Bob leaning out waving both arms and trying to do thumbs-up at the same time.

"He's loving it," smiled El Chano. "Ever since his rescue, he has wanted to ride in one of those things again. Hope he finds what he is looking for."

It was almost dusk when the roar of the big, black bird returned. This time Bob had a grin plastered on his face that he would probably never wash off. He wanted to run; he even wanted to dance, but the black boot prevented anything but a fast walk to Luis and El Chano. He embraced them both, tears starting to well in his eyes.

"We found it, we found it! We didn't land, but I drew kind of a map. I didn't want it to look like there was anyone poking around until we got there to investigate. Besides, it is getting dark, and the pilot had to get back to the base. What a ride, boys, what a ride."

They checked out the shack, and this time brought along a tarp canopy to use as an extension. They learned that the closed-in space did not allow for the evening breezes. In fact they all felt they would rather sleep under the tarp than inside the cramped, airless shack.

"Whew, this is much better" said El Chano. "We will all breath better tonight. Now, how does Spam sound for dinner?"

The fire was built, the cast iron skillet was brought out, the span was cut, the eggs were ready for frying, and the store bought biscuits were ready for heating. There were three hungry men, and one could only hope there was enough to satisfy them. Of course, there was a large bag of donuts, just in case.

"The beer," yelled Chano "Who packed the beer?"

Luis smiled, "It's in the back seat! Under the sleeping bags. There's a cooler there. It should be perfect."

Well, now it was perfect. Each man chowed his spam, but the brew that washed it down made all the difference in the world. Yes, it was perfect.

There were no sounds except for a distant coyote, and a possible rabbit scurrying here and there. There was a welcomed breeze that lulled them to sleep, and in the morning, Luis surprised them all to the sizzle of bacon frying in the pan. He even scrambled the eggs and made an omelet of sorts, folded over some cheddar that he had shredded himself. That and leftover biscuits made it perfect, once again. They loaded up the jeep, anticipating an over-nighter in the hills. Bob got out his map, got his bearings, and in his most western voice, yelled "forward ho!"

"Westward ho," corrected El Chano, and they churned up desert sand once again with no road to guide them.

This time they had a larger jeep to hold the equipment they discovered they would need. Experience is always the best teacher. Both El Chano and Bob felt much better prepared for this trip, even if their arch enemy was over the next ridge.

El Chano was driving, Bob was pouring over his map, and Luis bounced happily along in the back seat.

"There's our mushroom," pointed Bob. "Now, according to my calculations we veer to the right and follow the base of the mountain. I figure in about an hour we will find an opening, probably an old river bed, that cuts through the mountain and should bring us to a large valley behind it, complete with a lake and small river; sure looked great from up there," he pointed,

"Then what?" asked El Chano. "Was there any sign of life; any ranch or structure?"

"You got it, but we didn't see it on the first swipe. I had a hunch that this would be a great place for a ranch, so I asked the pilot to swing around again and go a little further in to the valley.

The first thing I saw were the brown dots that were moving. Cattle, boys. It was a real working ranch. We soon came upon a barn and nestled in a grove of beech, was the ranch house. Prettiest picture I ever saw. We couldn't see anyone around and didn't want to alert anyone if there was, so we followed the road that headed in the opposite direction and finally hooked up with a real road running north and south. Now everything made sense. I even assigned Higgins, at county, to find out who owns that ranch. Real pretty spot, and according to the map I found, there is actually a town of sorts, about another 50 miles south of here. Amazing."

"The theory being," continued El Chano, is that our killer was stalking us, went to his base ranch, got on his motorcycle, with the intention of leaving us on the desert floor to feed the vultures."

"Almost worked, too," said Bob, "but Chano, here, saved the day as a good novel would say, and came roaring to the rescue in a big, black helicopter. All I have to show for the adventure is a broken ankle, and this damn black boot."

They all laughed together and passed the canteen. "Plenty of water, this time," said Luis. "No way we can be skuttled. I even hid the other large water container." He laughed, "Now all I have to do is remember where I hid it." They all laughed together, each one hoping that Luis was pulling their leg. No one dared ask.

Stories were told amidst the laughter, and the time flew by Before they knew it, Bob stood up in the jeep and pointed. "There it is, turn, turn!"

El Chano left a trail of flying sand as he nearly missed the turn. Well, anyone could miss it. There was no road and, of course, a lot of boulders to navigate. They finally found themselves on the soft floor of a dry river bed that probably flowed during the rainy season when the mountain tributaries emptied their load.

"You know what?" asked Luis, "if we come here after the rainy season I bet we would find gold nuggets just lying about. I would love to test my theory. In fact, I heard of a tourist in Redding, that stopped his car, walked down to the river right in town, and picked up a nugget. See, it can happen."

"We will have to watch for the rainy season," said El Chano, and try it out. That is if this damn case is ever solved. Don't look at me like that, Bob. Also, do you think we'll find our suspect here?"

"I guess anything is possible, but we kept the trip top

secret. Even so, this guy has a sixth sense. I just don't know."

"OK, mastermind," said El Chano, as he stopped the jeep, with the ranch now within throwing distance, "where to first?"

Let's get in the house and do a thorough search. Luis, you take the barn, I don't know what we are looking for; just use your instincts. Go for it."

Luis patted his 38, then crossed what he thought looked like a landing strip for a small cub, and entered the barn, which turned out to be much more than an ordinary barn.

He whistled as he stood there trying to identify some of the equipment. He couldn't. There were horizontal pile driers, or so it seemed. He began to wonder if there was a larger gold nine around that needed shoring up. "There must be," he whispered to himself as he continued down the barn. Then he saw it; a helmet with a dark visor on a post near the rear entrance. He had a feeling there would be fingerprints, but even if there were, what would that prove? Someone that lived or worked here had a motorcycle. "It might fly in my mind, but not in the jury's," he said to himself. There just had to be something else."

Then he looked down at the soft dirt floor. There it was, tire tracks. He started to follow them, and it took him around the outside of the barn and in a straight line toward the opening in the canyon. In fact, the tracks ran right up to the jeep, and continued beyond. He whistled again, and ran inside to find Bob and El Chano.

That's when it happened. When the shot rang out it seemed a distance away, and by the time it hit Luiss' shoulder, it seemed like a different bullet. He went down and El Chano and Bob came running. Another shot, and then another, and then two more.

"Are we under siege?" yelled Bob, as he ran toward Luis. He just happened to look over at the jeep as he ran and could see the destination of the last two bullets; two flat tires

He bent over Luis, who was now unconscious. "He's got a powerful long-distance riffle," yelled Bob. "He can pick us off easily. He's got our tires, so we had better get Luis in the house and hunker down. The shots came from that short rise behind the twin palms. If you can get to the jeep, there is a riffle next to the walki-talkies. Yeh, I may have been prepared, but he still has a bead on us. Try for the riffle, and cover me while I carry Luis inside. Ready?"

El Chano ran, dropped commando-style and rolled to the jeep. He grabbed the riffle and started shooting. Bob managed Luis over his shoulder and ran for the door. El Chano kept firing. When Bob was inside, Chano picked up the talkies and sprinted to the door, just as another bullet splintered the frame. They slammed the door and threw the bolt.

"You check the windows and doors, Chano, while I see to Luis. Got to stop the bleeding.

Bob found some bedding that he quickly cut and tore into strips. Then he began cleaning the wound with some hydrogen peroxide he found in the kitchen. Soon Luis was dry and wrapped. Bob looked around for some whisky and found a quarter of a bottle in the cupboard. When Luis finally opened his eyes, Bob propped him up and gave him a swig. Luis nodded. "More," he said, and Bob complied.

El Chano came back in the room and smiled at Luis, now sitting up on the couch,

"OK, Bob, here's the thing. Too damn many windows for us to cover. There is only one other door in the kitchen, but we can't be everywhere. I found a window on the second floor where I can reach the roof. I figure if I plant myself up there, I could pick off anyone approaching the house. :

They looked over at Luis who was anxious to speak. "Boss, there's a helmet in the barn that matches your description, and guess what, tire tracks leading to where we came into the canyon, Also in the barn is a lot of heavy, mining equipment. We hit the jackpot. Do we have a plan?"

"He looks like the cat who ate the canary," commented El Chano. OK, Bob, let's have it."

Bob picked up the walkie-talkies and smiled. "These are on loan from the Air Force. All I have to do is call in our location and they will be here. Didn't want to be stranded again. If the jeep is disabled, we will be airlifted out in style."

"I will call while you secure the premises," smiled Bob. "Shouldn't be too long. I will also tell our seals where the bushwhacker is hiding. Yeh, these guys are the best there is, and since this is a large scale murder case, and we are on mostly federal land, so close to the base, with no law enforcement within 200 miles: we have back-up. Wow!"

Everyone's adrenaline was running on high now. Even Luis was feeling no pain.

They could now hear El Chano's footsteps on the roof, followed by a couple of rounds of gunfire, as well as return fire that they hoped wouldn't hit its mark.

There was more fire and more return fire. "Will the ammo hold out?" asked Luis, starting to look worried again.

"El Chano must have seen the extra box I packed. I think we have enough, but he will have to gauge it. Now, I have to finish this call, I'm connected

"This is Bravo Bob. Pinned down in the river canyon that Stevens marked on the map. Shooter has a long range riffle north near twin palms. One man down. Jeep disabled. Need to evacuate. Over.

"Bravo force on the way. Can you hold for 20 minutes?"

"Holding. We have one man on the roof with a riffle."

Following periods of silence, El Chano let off another round followed by return fire.

"Why does he wait so long between rounds?" asked Luis,

"I would rather hear the gunfire."

"First of all," answered Bob, "he wants to conserve on ammo. Second he wants the enemy to know we are still able to defend ourselves and will take him out if we have the chance."

Luis smiled, "Thanks Bob. Say, do we have any water? I think ours is all in the jeep."

"Since this was our killer's home base, you would think there would be some water around. Hold down the couch while I go in the kitchen." Bob was surprised when he opened the door to the fridge. It was fully stocked, and that included beer. He smiled, but chose the bottled water instead. Before he brought it in to Luis, he noticed a door in the floor at the end of the kitchen.

"Worth exploring," he thought, "I just hope there are no more bodies buried down there."

Luis drank his fill as Bob walked over to the window and carefully pulled back the curtain. A shot immediately rang out and sent glass shards flying, one large one landing in his forearm.

"I am not going to say it, boss," smiled Luis

"You don't have to. Guess I was starting to feel a little cocky." He backed away from the window and joined Luis on the couch and pulled the shard from his arm, dabbing the blood with his handkerchief.

That's when they heard it. There was something in the kitchen. Bob pulled out his 38 and stealthily tiptoed to the kitchen. He saw the back door slightly ajar and the end of a rope swinging in the breeze.

He ran to the front, opened the door and yelled, "Behind you!" They heard one riffle shot, then one bump, then two, then what looked like a sack of potatoes fall past the broken window. The sack lay in the doorway so Bob grabbed its arm and pulled it inside and closed the door.

He was slight of build and wearing the motorcycle helmet. It was obvious he was dead as the blood saturated his shirt from the neck down, almost like the throat had been slit. Kind of poetic, he thought, then regretted it. "No way to die, for anyone," said Bob as he glanced over at Luis.

"Boss, this doesn't look like a guy. Let's see who it is, or was, that is."

Bob gently removed the helmet and long ringlets of brown hair cascaded to the floor and around the now white face.

"Oh, my God," exclaimed Luis. "It's Gladys, Manuel's daughter. Isn't she only 19?"

Bob stepped back and took a breath. "Greed has no age limit, 18 or 19, young or old. They also call it gold fever. What a waste."

"You kind of thought, all along, the master-killer wasn't working alone. boss," said Luis. You were right, but I would never have guessed Gladys."

They both stopped to listen. No more gun shots.

"The shooter must have seen her go down and took off," said Bob. He called up to El Chano, "Do you think he is gone?"

"Coming down," Chano yelled back.

In just a minute he stood in the living room looking down at what remained of Gladys. "I didn't mean to do that to her. All I did was turn, see the pistol, and fired. Damn!"

Bob left the room and grabbed three beers from the fridge. "This is by no means a celebration. Or, maybe just a little one for just being alive. Thanks, El Chano." They raised their bottles and clicked; a sound that ushered in the roar of the helicopter. The Seals had arrived.

Bob was holding out his shield so they wouldn't be shot as the seals stormed through the door. Yep, it was awesome and worth writing home about. Four of the bravest in the US Military, fully regaled, and now pointing their automatics at the occupants of the room; everyone held their breath.

The shield was checked, and Bob began his explanation of the morning's events. Gladys was checked for signs of life, then wrapped in a blanket and placed aboard the copter. Luis followed and would be taken immediately to Anaconda General.

Bob and El Chano looked at each other and nodded.

"Captain," said Bob, addressing the senior officer, "we have not completed our mission. The mastermind escaped, and we believe there is a mine close by with enough evidence to hang him.

"I understand, Sir. Anything we can do to help?"

Bob thought for a minute, "You know, Luis needs a doctor, but I think another 15 minutes one way or another wouldn't hurt him. Just one sweep of the ranch looking for tracks to somewhere in those hills, would help? It would take us forever on foot."

"Let's do it!" said the Captain, as he waved his hand in a rotary fashion and the helicopter blades began to roar.

They all loaded on board and the sweep began. They first circled the house and barn looking for a road toward the hills. They followed one toward the furthest peak.

The Captain saw it first and pointed. Everyone strained to look, holding on for dear life, not wanting to fall. The copter took a wide turn and headed straight for the mountain wall. Everyone held their breath.

All of a sudden they were face to face with the solid rock of the mountain.

"Down there, look!" yelled El Chano. There is a road meandering up the south end."

The copter headed south and followed the road. Everyone in the helicopter cheered when the side of the granite opened, and a gaping black hole lay before them. The copter hovered for a minute then circled back.

It was an excited crew that landed back at the ranch. There were handshakes all around and promises for several rounds of beer when this case was concluded.

Bob and El Chano had a bitter-sweet taste as they watched them fly away. "Now we get to work, and I can only hope that our mysterious killer is long gone.

The Seals had repaired one of the tires and replaced the other with the spare. Bob loaded their supplies and they set off once more on their mission to seal the fate of one of the worst killers either of them had ever encountered.

It took them at least 45 minutes to reach the road that meandered up the mountain. They took it as far as it would go and parked it where other vehicles had parked before. The trail narrowed and it was easy to see work had been done to widen it for the heavy equipment that Luis had found in the barn.

With their back packs loaded with water and equipment for sample mining, they continued down the path. Once at the opening they switched on their helmets. If either one were asked, they would definitely say they were starting to have a damn good time.

"You take the right side and I'll take the left," said Bob. "Let's see if there is really gold in 'them-thar-hills.'" They hadn't gone three feet when both men were on their knees brushing off nuggets. Three, four, five, ten, they counted.

Neither one could speak, but finally El Chano did, "Bob, this is the mother load of mother loads. Temptation is really gnawing at me. If we just pocketed a couple of these, who the hell would know?"

"We would," said Bob, soberly. "But, I have the same temptations, especially with a wedding coming up. Let's check it all out and then get back to camp. I'm starving for a burnt slice of that glorious spam."

They put all their nuggets into one bag, looked at each other for a moment, then just tossed it in their back pack.

"Oh, well," said El Chano. "You know what they say, 'Easy come!'"

They knew they would have to spend the night, so the preparations for dinner and sleeping were slow and easy. Actually, they both felt they deserved a respite. By the time the last piece of spam and eggs was consumed, they were beginning to yawn. "I just had a thought," said Bob, "we checked and checked all the claims and mines registered, and this mother-load wasn't listed. How could that be, especially one as rich as that?"

"Just suppose," said El Chano, "that our killer and his partner were afraid of being found out, so to speak. Imagine what would happen if others knew of this mine? Why, this valley would be crawling with prospectors, and who wouldn't kill for a piece of action in that mine. My sense is that they felt they could keep it a secret until the time was right."

"I see your drift," responded Bob. "I also see that if the mine is not registered, it is presently open to all prospectors. Are you a prospector, Chano? I know I can't be one because I am a county employee, but you are eligible."

El Chano scratched his head. "Let's pack up now and be ready to leave at first light. By the way, where is the Assayers Office, or the BLM, or wherever old prospectors go to register a claim? Drop me off when we get back."

Chapter 20

Hell (a killer)
Hath No Fury...

Lieutenant Bob (Roberto) Mendoza walked into headquarters and was surprised at the reaction. Everyone stopped what they were doing and actually stood and applauded. There were also a few whistles and hoopla's. He bowed, glanced over their heads and was surprised to see Manuel Cardoza sitting patiently in the only chair adjacent to his desk.

When he reached the desk Manuel looked up. "They think you are a hero. I want you to know I don't think so. She was only 19 years old. What could she know of the world. She didn't deserve to die, not that way, with a bullet through her neck. I just came from the morgue to identify the body. She was so beautiful, and was actually in the top 10 in her class. We were even thinking of her going to UCLA. She was accepted last year, but I think she got in with the wrong crowd. What happens to dreams, Lieutenant, where do they go?"

Bob was not ready for this, but, he asked himself, "Is anybody?"

"I am so sorry, Manuel, but I don't think dreams go anywhere. They are just replaced with new ones. And sometimes those new dreams are tarnished with things like greed. I don't know how it happens, Manuel, and I'm sorry, but there is such a thing as gold fever, and all that wealth can provide. She probably listened to someone who told her how her life would change with pots of gold. She wasn't the first, Manuel, and she won't be the last."

Manuel just sat for a minute with his face in his hands; then he looked up. "You were there; did you kill her?"

Bob shook his head. Does it really matter now? She didn't suffer, if that's what you want to know. Not with a shot like that. Just remember, Manuel, she had a gun, too. Now, you realize, don't you, that the person who got her into this is the one who is ultimately responsible for her death. If you know anything, like who she was hanging out with, don't take it to your grave. Let us catch him. He is ruthless, Manuel. He has too many notches in his belt now to stop killing if he thinks he needs to. Who is he, Manuel?"

Their eyes met and Bob could see the pain. He felt sorry for Manuel, but also knew that he was a prime candidate for the next Taco Tuesday murder if he didn't tell what he knew.

"Do you want me to put a man on you? I think you need protection."

Manuel shook his head. "No, what should I care if I live now, with my Gladys gone. No, but I want to be sure."

He rose, started to shake Bob's hand, but changed his mind. Head bowed, he just turned and walked out of the station. Several eyes followed his departure, most understanding his grief, and knowing full well that there was nothing they could do to help.

It took Bob all day to finish his reports, and he was anxious to get to the hospital to see Luis. He had, of course, talked to him on his cell, just long enough to know he and the nurses were getting along beautifully. "He is healing," smiled Bob to himself.

He called Stella to see if she was up to dinner, and she said she had already shopped and it would be ready about 7:00. Bob smiled to himself, a warmth had just covered his body; he knew he was one of the luckiest men in the world. He looked at his watch and saw there was enough time to stop at the hospital and then go home for a quick shower and change. Life was beautiful. Then he thought of Manuel and his mood changed. He saw the blood stained face of Gladys and his stomach jumped. He knew the killer was ruthless, and there was a gnawing deep inside that told him it wasn't over yet.

Once Bob stepped outside he took a deep breath and looked into the smiling face of El Chano standing beside a brand new grey and cream SUV,

"Yours?" asked Bob, barely able to spit out the words, knowing full well where the money came from to buy this monster.

"They have another one with your name on it if you want one; though maybe you better check with Stella, first."

El Chano saw the questions in Bob's eyes. "Yes, we own the mine. I not only staked a claim but also purchased about 10 acres of that piece of granite the mine is on. Also, my friend, those rocks I had assayed came to a total in currency of $330,000. We have a new bank account; yes, your name is on it. All you have to do is go down and sign."

Bob still couldn't speak. Finally, he walked over to El Chano and gave him a bear hug. There was even a tear in his eye.

He cleared his throat. "I am going over to see Luis. Want to come?"

"Hop in," said Chano. "We go in style. Oh, watch your boot on that first step."

They both stood outside room 235 because there was hardly room inside. There were about five nurses gathered around Luis's bed; not for health reasons, but each one flirting to get his attention.

Bob looked over at El Chano and shrugged. "Be right back."

He walked in the room carrying two large balloons, tied them to the railing of the bed and said, "He's all yours, ladies."

Once back in the hall, he and Chano checked in at the nurses station to see when Luis would be discharged. "Tell Romeo, in there, that I will be back at 11:00 tomorrow morning to wheel him home. That is, if he wants to go."

El Chano was thinking about Sydney and the prospect of taking her out in the new ride and maybe for dinner. When they reached the car he dialed and she was more than pleased to comply with the plan. He was beaming.

Bob gave a chuckle and congratulated him on his success. "It looks like we each have a night with the ladies, but I seem to have forgotten one thing. I told Stella I would propose again when this case was solved, but that means I will be engaged. El Chano, that means a ring, doesn't it?"

El Chano laughed, "Usually does, amigo, but it is not too late. The case is not over, and you have time to buy a ring. Ha! With our new social standing, you can give 'her hearts desire.'"

"No problem, there is time to find out. Didn't she ever give you any clues?"

"I'm too dense to know if she did. Oh, there is that one time we were in a restaurant, an English Pub, to be exact, and they had a poster with Princess Di holding a glass of champagne where you could see her ring. She did say that diamonds and sapphires were her favorite combination."

"There you are; you have answered your own question. Here is the condo, go have yourself a great evening. Tomorrow, the bank."

Bob was elated as he entered his condo. After his bank signing tomorrow, he would check the jewelry store.

"The size," he said out-loud in the elevator, and embarrassed the woman standing next to him. He took courage and asked, "How do I get the size of my girlfriends finger for an engagement ring?"

She laughed sympathetically, as the elevator reached her floor. "My boy, you simply ask."

"Why didn't I think of that? I guess guys always think there is a subtle way to do things that we should instinctively know from birth." He laughed, "I guess I don't have to know everything. No, it will be more fun learning life together with Stella."

He wished he had at least stopped for flowers since she was cooking dinner. He looked at his watch. There was time. Shower, grey slacks and blue shirt, then the market down the street. "Hope they have some pink roses left."

This time when he stood outside the door, she didn't hesitate. His hands were full of flowers, but hers weren't. On her tip-toes, she reached up and kissed him. He kissed her back.

She then took the flowers and his arm and led him inside, looking at his boot as thy went.

"Is there any pain," she asked.

He shook his head "No, it is more of an annoyance than anything. It actually feels good when I take it off."

"Then let's take it off," she whispered. "Dinner is about an hour out. Oh, I have some champagne already cooled."

Well, of all the things that Bob could have imagined, this wasn't one of them. The last time they were in this room it was in a moment of passion with no time to think or plan. He really wanted the next time to be more romantic. He wasn't sure just what that meant, but he felt if they went slower, he would have more time to show her how much he loved her. Hell, what did he know. He had two sips of champagne, his boot and shirt were already off, and the sheets were rolled back from the bed. She was already in with nothing to protect her loveliness.

"Damn!" he said as he threw all caution and romance to the wind and dove right in. "Yep," he whispered as he rolled over. "This may be as romantic as it gets."

They both giggled, as they snuggled closer. "If this isn't romance, my dear, I don't know what is."

"I was kind of thinking of talking about feelings and maybe just holding hands. Crazy, huh?" asked Bob.

She thought for a minute, then tears filled her eyes. "Can we start over. Let's get dressed and sit in the other room. I think I would very much like to do that.

And so, it was a very romantic evening, after all. Each one got to know a little more about the other, about points of endearment, places where their lives touched; like deep inside where nobody hardly ever goes. They found they were soul-mates, after all, and they both felt a closeness they had not had before.

Yes, viva la romance.

Meanwhile, across town, El Chano and Sydney were enjoying dinner behind the palm at Luigi's. She listened intently as he related their experience with the Seals and with the difficulty of reconciling his having to shoot the girl.

"She was only 19," explained El Chano, "but I don't know if I will ever get over it,"

"But, Chano," pleaded Sydney, "she may have been a silly child, but she was playing adult games. She would have killed you and probably would not have given it a second thought. You were not responsible for her death. She brought it on herself."

"I know you're right, at least the reasonable side of my brain says so; however, my heart is giving me problems."

"I can understand that, but if I were you, I would concentrate on catching the monster who was responsible for so many deaths, including hers."

"Thanks Sydney, you definitely are the voice of reason and sanity; I needed to hear that. Thank you."

"How about coffee at my place," she offered. "Besides you look beat. I don't think you have recovered from the desert."

"You are probably right, and I also know you have a few bones to clean up in that bone-yard of yours. I know I know, archeology is serious work, and I really am overwhelmed with your ability. Seriously, I am. As they stood outside the restaurant he held her close, kissed both cheeks, and then her mouth.

"See I am really not that tired, after all."

She was about to kiss him back when someone came running down the street towards them wearing a motorcycle helmet. El Chano was about to pull her out of the way when he saw the street light reflecting on the blade that he held over his head. Sydney saw it too and screamed. She dropped to the ground just as the knife swung. Fortunately, it did not find her neck but instead her upper arm that she had raised to protect herself.

Chano moved quickly and flung himself at the assailant, but the knife swung wide again and slashed his hand. As each one grabbed their own wounds the monster disappeared into the shadows and soon the sound of a motorcycle was heard speeding away

By now Sydney was unconscious and was bleeding heavily. It was difficult, but Chano managed a 911 on his cell. The paramedics were the first to arrive and tended to Sydney's wound that was too deep, and would need stitches, Also, because of her loss of blood, the hospital was the best place for her.

El Chano was also bandaged, but decided to accompany Sydney in the ambulance. This time his right hand dialed another familiar number.

"Bob, is that you? Sydney and I were just attacked on the street and are headed to the hospital. I am leaving my lovely new vehicle at Luigi's. And guess who I think the assailant was? He was wearing a helmet and made his get-away on a motorcycle. Yep, I really think it was him. Yes, I thought you would like to get on it right away."

Bob quickly explained what happened to Stella, then called downtown. The wheels of justice were now in motion. Romance would have to wait.

All the way downtown Bob kept thinking that this attack was the killer's way of getting even. "One of his own was killed, so why not make her killer pay with the life of his girl? Oh, good grief, am I actually starting to think like him?" Bob shook his head, but he also realized that this could be their edge. "Just maybe we can use his MO against him. We've got to stop the next murder," he said out loud; Taco Tuesday or not."

Bob was deep in thought, then he brightened, "I know I am right about the pay back. I remember the old saying about 'anger hath no fury like a woman scorned.' Well, this killer has enough anger and fury for everyone in the Pelican Bay Penitentiary."

Chapter 21

The Fat Lady Didn't Sing (yet)

Bob was at his desk the next morning, just fumbling through papers he didn't even see. All he could see was Manuel sitting in the chair he occupied the other day. Manuel knows too much, he thought, and he doesn't realize how dangerous that is with a killer that has no regard for human life, except his own, of course.

He did put a man on Manuel, but he knew from experience that if a person didn't want help, it was pretty hard to protect him.

He slid his spiral over and decided to get organized. It was difficult because he kept picturing El Chano with his bandaged hand, and Sydney, who was given a room in the hospital because she lost so much blood from the slash in her shoulder and arm. She looked so helpless, her expression so incredulous as she shook her head and said how much safer she felt in Israel. Yes, incredulous, is the word for the comparison. Even so, she was adamant about returning to Jerusalem and the dig near the Mount of

Olives. She turned her face away and closed her eyes. That was the signal for El Chano and I to leave.

Once outside in the hall, Chano's faced turned red with anger. "Look what happened to her. I was right beside her and I couldn't prevent the stabbing. Hell, Bob, I'm no damn good at anything, if I can't even take care of my gal on a dinner date. Now she is determined to go back to Israel, and I don't blame her at all."

"You are being too hard on yourself. I don't know of anybody who could have done any better. Look, you are both still alive, and she will have a story to tell her grandchildren, some day. Come on, amigo, do you want to stop for a brew?"

El Chano shook his head. No, my amigo, what I want is to catch this monster. There has to be a way. I know, I know, he is as clever as hell, and has gotten away with at least 6 murders. I would like to lay a trap for him."

Bob sat there thinking. "I like your idea of setting a trap. Do you have time to come to the office, right now? I am picking Luis up first, then I'll send out for food. I have an idea."

Of course, the idea of setting a trap for the killer brightened Chano's day. They both sat down at the mahogany desk with pen and pad and began to list the bazaar acts of this murderer. How in the world could any of this be used against him? "Or, maybe we could use some of his antics to trap him?" exlaimed Chano.

They both wrote furiously, listing everything from the extravagant preparation in the locked stall to the grotesque way she was murdered. The killer went to a lot of trouble drilling the holes and creating the illusion of a locked stall mystery. Chano laughed at his own synopsis, but the more he thought about it the more he realized that the planning that went into the murder was quite extensive.

Then there were the snakes. "Why the snakes?" Bob asked himself? "There just had to be a reason. A person, killer or not, does not go to all the trouble of procuring three snakes and setting them loose in a restaurant. What was the killer doing at that time? Was he covering his tracks in some way by creating a diversion? Yes, that had to be it. He was creating a diversion; but for what?"

Then there was Juan's murder. Why, again? Yes, he was Clare's agent in California and probably knew her better than anyone. But, what did he know? What did she know? Too many unanswered questions. Also, as in Clare's murder, there was too much blood.

True, Bob discovered that the blood bank downtown was robbed, and the blood type was the same. He supposed that was easy to discover, but again, why?

El Chano looked down at his pad and discovered there was just one word written there, 'snakes.' Again, why did he write that when there were so many other bazaar elements?

He laughed to himself. The snakes scared everyone because they looked deadly.

"I wonder how knowledgeable the killer was about snakes? Hmmm, maybe we can run with this."

El Chano looked up expectantly at Bob. "Just going over the case, listing all the peculiarities and looking for a crack," he explained. Let' s compare notes, two geniuses are always better than one."

The word 'blood' was the word that intrigued Bob. "Why so much, and why stage it again in Juan's murder?" he asked El Chano. "Was there a significance here that escapes me?"

The second word was theatrical. "Yes, everything about this case reminded Bob of either a movie or a play down at the dinner theatre. "Just seems to me," he ventured, "that this killer had to be connected with, or had a love for all things show-bizz. Worth looking into."

When he finished his list, Bob was surprised at his selections. Blood topped the list, followed by theatre, organization, intelligence, alibi, timing, and alibi again. The last thing on the list was snakes. He laughed as he tried to reason why the snakes made the list at all, Yes, it was entertaining, once they knew the snakes were not their poisonous counterparts. Even when Rosa was bit, as was another man, it still had the aura of theatre.

"I keep coming back to the word theatre," Bob said, "I felt all along that I was watching a performance; that I was being entertained. Good God, so I was. I believe that was the killers' intention all along. But why? It had to be so he could establish an alibi, and that he could, like a conjurer, saw the lady in half while he gathered up the real clues of the murder."

"What were the real clues?" Bob asked. "I fell for this slight of hand nonsense, too. I didn't hear the scream, which would have been blood curdling, as her throat was being cut. OR WOULD IT? Bob jumped up and ran over to Luis.

"Luis, play along with me. I am going to pretend that I am slitting your throat and I want you to try to scream. Not just an ordinary scream, but a scream they would hear outside on the street. My razor is going to be this pencil. Yes, I am using the eraser end. Ready now, here we go."

Chano moved closer to watch the demonstration, understanding where Bob was going.

"Do I try to fight you off? I just don't want to be a clay pigeon."

"No Luis, you are not a pigeon, you are a victim, and the killer is about to slash your throat. Now, are you ready?"

Bob dug the eraser deep into Luis's throat and drew it across from ear to ear. Luis screamed. "Louder. Luis, let's try again. So, Bob drew the eraser deeply across his neck once again. Luis screamed again. Some of the police in the room looked up, but most of them continued with their work.

"Boss, it was hard to scream with that eraser pushing on my vocal cords. Hurt some, too."

"Of course it did. The scream that everyone said they heard was not the real scream, if there was one. It was theatre."

"It was probably his accomplice on tape through speakers somewhere in the dining room," said El Chano. "There is no other way it could have been that loud. I even question whether or not the poor woman was able to scream at all after I saw the condition of her throat."

"Speakers!" yelled Bob excitedly. "El Chano, you're a genius."

"Wow!" exclaimed Chano. "I see it. Now I see the reason for the snakes."

They looked at each other and smiled. "The old conjurers trick," said Bob. "Watch the snakes while I get my speakers. A real slight of hand. But why? There was no apparent need for the scream."

"There had to be a reason," said Chano. "This guy doesn't do anything without it being part of his master plan."

Both men sat quietly. Each one knew there was an answer; it just escaped them for the moment. Bob pulled forward his pad and passed it over to Chano. "I was doodling. Trying to put together some ideas; thinking there was a clue in here somewhere."

El Chano chuckled, "Did you realize that you wrote one word twice?"

Bob pulled the pad back and laughed. "Chano, what did I ever do without you? I said it before, you are a genius. Alibi, right?"

"Alibi! Everyone was so sure, you said, that the scream gave you the time of the murder. Time, Bob. What if she was murdered long before the scream, so the killer was able to position himself in a visible location so he would have that alibi with a room full of people to corroborate it."

Bob nodded his head in agreement. "I don't think I have ever been up against what they call, a 'master criminal,' before. It is not going to be easy to pin this guy down. I did have an idea, though. I just started working it out, but do you see the word snake on my doodle list? Well, it seems like he is somewhat of an expert. How else would he know how to choose a snake that looked just like a deadly variety, but was totally harmless?"

"Good observation, Bob," agreed Chano. "Are you suggesting that we turn some snakes on him?"

"Don't I wish. Maybe, but whatever we do, it has to be part of our master plan, and it has to rattle him to the point where he will make a fatal mistake."

"Well," said Chano, "if you are looking for a snake expert, it isn't me. What do we do now?"

"We just find the expert." Bob signaled Mable at the front desk, "Get me the City Zoo, Reptile Department."

El Chano sat sipping on his coffee, wishing he had something to go with it. Hunger was starting to gnaw.

Bob finally made a connection. "Hello, this is Will Morgan, how can I help you?"

"I need your help to catch a killer. This is Lieutenant Mendoza, Homicide. When would you have time to discuss the case?"

"This is one of those hectic days, Lieutenant. I can see you during lunch at our café near the lions. How about noon?"

"See you at noon, and bring your manual on California's poisonous snakes."

"I suppose you are going to want samples. We have a few."

"How about some 'look-alikes'?"

"I can fill that order, too. See you later, but no snakes are allowed in the café," he laughed.

"What happened, Bob, you look too happy."

"We are having lunch at the Zoo with the Herpetologist, that's snake expert, to you. They also have samples. Now, all we have to do is set the stage, and as quickly as possible. You see, I am trying to prevent another murder."

"Well, this is Friday; Tuesday is close by. What do you think?"

"Taco Tuesday, huh? Yeah, let's see if we can put it together."

"Yeah," said El Chano. "It's not over yet; she hasn't sung."

Chapter 22

More Jelly Donuts

The roar of the lions was louder than they expected; the café was positioned above and to the left of their compound, which was great for viewing, but if the beasts were being fed or just felt rumbustious, the sound carried right into the dining room. By the time Will arrived, they were moved into their inside cages and all was silent.

"Must be nap time," teased Bob. Will just shook his head.

"Nope, they have scheduled medication for flee infestation. Crazy, huh? Now, what can I do for you reptile lovers?"

Bob outlined the drama created by the snakes that were released the night of the murder. They looked deadly and two customers were actually bitten. Scared them silly."

"Sounds like the snakes were more scared than the patrons. They probably felt they were under attack and took a bite of the first leg they saw."

Bob passed over a picture of one of the snakes and Will nodded his head. "Yep, we have those guys. We also have two of their counterpart in glass enclosures." He pulled out a pamphlet. "See the only difference is that orange spot on the head. This is how you tell whether or not they are poisoness."

Bob looked at El Chano, and Chano returned the look.

"Would the Zoo possibly consent to loaning the police department three of these beauties after you paint those spots on their heads?"

Will burst out laughing. "You're serious, aren't you?"

"Very serious. This killer has no compulsion about who his victim is, or how many there are. This is in the strictest confidence, but I want you to take a look at our candidate"

Bob passed over the picture and watched Will's face. It was not what he expected.

Good God, this is Arnold, Arnold Stravinsky. He worked here at the zoo for about a year in my department. He had studied zoology, more particularly, Herpetology, you know, the study of reptiles. Is this his real name, by the way?"

"As far as we know," said Bob, "he may have several aliases. We will find out before Tuesday. So, is it possible to prepare the slithering beauties in time?"

"If you mean paint the orange dot on their heads and get the approval from the boss, I think we can."

"Tell your boss we can always confiscate the reptiles, but I would rather not. Anyway, let me know if you have any trouble. Now, my partner here, and I, have to write the script for this little performance. Thank you, Will, it has been a pleasure. Oh, I would invite you to attend, but I don't want our suspect to recognize you and get wise to our little plan,"

After Will left, Bob and El Chano sat quietly, deep I thought.

"Little plan, huh," teased Chano.

Bob smiled, "Well, I have to admit it is in the brain-works stage, but I was so sure that between us we would come up with something. I want to get back to the office; I can think better at my desk. Come on, let's devise a plan more devious, and by far, more clever, than any of our advisories. We can do it, El Chano."

Si, senior. Lead the way!"

Once they were back at the dark, mahogany desk, that had seen many better days, they both sat with yet, another cup of coffee.

"How can you drink so much bean?" asked Chano.

"Habit, I guess. That, and it gives me something to do as I think. So much better with a jelly donut, though."

They both laughed, but Chano licked his lips. "We need dessert and it will give me something to do while you get the ball in motion. Two more jelly donuts coming up."

"Make that three," came a voice from across the room. It was Luis, and he was smiling and waving the arm without the sling.

El Chano gave him a thumbs up, and was out the door, as Luis walked over to Bob's desk.

"I was at the city zoo, and they have snakes," Bob smiled. "I want to corner our killer in a little drama that will make him feel the walls are closing in on him. Actually, we will be closing in."

"How are we going to pull it off, boss?"

"We will have another gathering at the restaurant on the next Taco Tuesday; only this time I will position them in smaller tables like those on the night of the murder. No celebrity table, because I want them to see and feel what the customers experienced that night. We are going to direct a play, Luis, much like the one that our killer produced that night. He had everything planned down to providing for his own alibi. He was good. The play was flawless. I only hope we can do as well."

"So, this is where the snakes come in?" asked Luis as he retrieved his coffee and pulled up a chair.

Exactly, but first we have to have the murder. Remember that the scream was loud and got everyone's attention. Stella even made a note of the time, just in case. That time, Luis, was the killer's motive because he was sitting in plain sight at the celebrity table. You have to give this guy credit,"

"So, you are saying that it was all smoke and mirrors, that the victim was not killed at that time. That means he had an accomplice."

"Yes, and unfortunately for her, she was killed while we were out in the desert. She was shot while aiming her gun at El Chano."

"OK, but how did she scream that loudly so everyone could hear? I couldn't when you pulled that little experiment."

"She didn't," said El Chano, as he walked in the room waving a bag of jelly donuts.

"Well, what the hell did she do?" asked Luis as he grabbed for the bag.

"I believe the speaker had already been set up," explained Bob, "probably over by the stage. They must have had a signal and she turned on the tape. She was already in the parking lot making her escape before anyone thought to look around."

"Let me guess, said Luis. "The killer needed to remove the speaker before we arrived. Ah, the snakes."

"The prize goes to the gentleman in the sling" smiled El Chano

"How did he release the reptiles?"

"My guess," said El Chano, is that he walked over to the bar to refresh his drink, and on his way back he just happened to drop something, like a bag of snakes."

They all took time out to savor the donut and to think about their adaptation of the play.

"The part I am looking forward to is the snakes, even though the scream is going to unsettle him. You see Luis; we are getting snakes from the zoo that will look like their poisoness brothers. They will have the markings of a deadly reptile."

"Will the killer know that?' questioned Luis.

"You bet. In fact he actually worked for the zoo, and, believe it or not, with the reptiles."

"The guy is going to freak out when he sees them," Luis gasped. "What next, how do we proceed?"

"Well," said Bob, "he will be the only one, besides us, of course, that will know how deadly they are (or their look-alikes are). I believe his first instinct will be to run. We will be waiting for him and escort him back to the table. Then a handler from the zoo will round up the snakes."

"I think a nice touch," said El Chano, would be to have two nuggets from the mine on the table where he was sitting. He must feel the noose tightening by now."

I would like to see the motorcycle helmet appear on his seat or somewhere, when he returns, or maybe a photo of the victim we found buried in the mine. Either one, or both, I don't much care. He's a monster and deserves to be rattled as much as possible."

"Then there is the ring you got clonked on the head for," added Bob. How about we display that on the person who is going to play the corpse?"

"Hey, what about the bloody foot print at the scene of the second murder? Anything conclusive on that one?" asked Chano,

"Too many of those athletic shoes around, and I would guess that if they belonged to the killer, they would now reside in the county dump," said Bob.

"I think we can pull it off," said Luis, calmly, and I hope you will let me have a part."

Each man held out his hand, and they piled one upon the other. Now it was a pact. Now there was a determined, organized force to fight the enemy. They sat down and licked the last of their jelly donut.

Chapter 23

Making a List

The next day the trio was back at the mahogany desk with a brown bag filled with, not only jelly donuts, but also with ham sandwiches. The trio was concentrating on the names on Bob's list of suspects. El Chano pointed to the first name. "This guy, Manuel, is he considered a suspect or a potential victim? I can see him in either roll"

"I see your point," agreed Bob. "He seemed sincerely broken over his daughter's death, but that could be as a father, master criminal or not. It wouldn't be the first time there was a father and daughter team. I can see the possibilities. We are checking into both backgrounds now, and it seems that she studied zoology for a short time. He was into finance, but he also has knowledge of the reptile world through his daughter."

"What about the late Gladys, what is her history, besides snakes?" asked Luis. "I haven't seen that report."

"She does have a history. She moves around a lot. Her passport is like a travel brochure. We traced her from

Budapest to Tel Aviv, then back to London, and believe it or not, she hit Iceland before she landed at JFK."

"What does she do? She must have an occupation of some kind," commented Luis.

"Her Passport says she exports antiquities," explained Bob. "In fact, we discovered that she was detained in London for carrying undisclosed gold nuggets. That doesn't necessarily fall under the heading of antiquities; they are older. Ha!"

"She was the perfect accomplice. Too bad it ended so tragically."

"Next," continued Bob, we have Sylvia, the one who made quite a scene the night of the murder accusing Clare of killing her friend. Seems to me that murderers often try to involve others in the very crime they committed themselves. We are investigating. Also, she is a singer/dancer and travels a lot, both here and abroad. Seems to me she is in a position to mastermind this production with, of course, as many accomplices as she can recruit."

"I didn't want to bring it up, El Chano, but there is your brother to be considered. We locked him up for a few days as a person of interest because he blatantly lied to the officers. However, between us, he is no material for a master criminal."

Bob cleared his throat. "Lastly, and my second favorite after Manuel, is the manager, Don Diego. Now, he is in a position to set the stage here in the restaurant. He could easily have set up the lavatory apparatuses, and ordered the painting well in advance. He also has a background in mining at UNLV, as well as being in a position to acquire as many accomplices as he needed. Gladys was very accessible."

"That's true," agreed El Chano, "but that brings us back to Manuel; do we presently consider him a suspect or a potential victim?"

"I have a man on him for his protection, just in case," answered Bob. "If, as we once thought, he could be the next Taco Tuesday victim, we will try to protect him. However, if he is destined to be targeted because he knows for a certainty, through his late daughter, who the killer is, I have to admit we are up against it. Whoever the killer is, he is a mastermind, and that means we have to muster all our mental resources to outfox him,"

"I think that is the understatement of this entire case," added El Chano. "However, I have an idea, and I would like to share it with you geniuses. I really would like to set a trap. Yes, I know, we are trying to rattle this monster or monsterette; but what if we put in a mock corpse and have a murder of our own before the killer can get to his. I think that would stop him in his tracks and prevent him from continuing with his plans. Of course, we can always hope he will expose himself before that."

Bob looked over at Chano and Luis. "What do you think, partners?"

"I think we have to try just about anything at this point," nodded El Chano. Putting both plans in play at once may just do it. Otherwise. . ."

"Agreed," said Luis.

"Yes, otherwise" repeated Bob. "OK, I think we need to break for the day and resume tomorrow morning. I know, it's Sunday, but Tuesday is just a couple of days away. I think each of us needs reflection time; brain power time. Then we can come together and see what we came up with. Three heads are better, they say."

Do you want to donut it again or maybe stop at Mable's for a stack and eggs?"

The stack and eggs won.

Even Bob thought he needed some R n R before they resumed again, "A man just doesn't sit down and think, and then rush out and solve the world's problems. Damn, how does he do it. I know I'm tired, but all of us are tired. I think we've got the best team on the force, then why am I agonizing over this case. Why?" he yelled at himself. "Because two people were killed on Taco Tuesday, and another found buried, never meant to be found. Ha! And God knows how many more."

"Enough," he said to himself, "everybody has to take some quiet time, if for no other reason than to reflect and grab a pizza."

Bob didn't watch where he was going, and he momentarily forgot about his boot. A freight elevator opened in the sidewalk ahead of him and bumped his leg. His boot twisted, he turned and nearly fell into the dark hole. He caught the side of the opening with his hand and undoubtedly prevented disaster.

A man was sitting astride his motorcycle watching the event, and seeing an opportunity, revved the cycle, circled around, ran over Bob's boot, and sent him reeling into a hole that was now only two feet deep as the elevator rose and brought him to the surface. He just lay there looking up into the curious faces that all wondered how anybody could possibly find themselves in that peculiar position.

El Chano saw the crowd gather and ran over just in time to gather Bob off the filthy elevator floor, and escort him to his car. Not a word was spoken. None was needed.

Bob climbed into another elevator, the one that took him to his condo, and decided a shower was necessary before he did anything else. He didn't trust himself. Fatigue can be fatal, he whispered, as the steam from the shower billowed out into the bedroom. After a good 15 minutes, some bath soap and a brush, he emerged a new man, but in need of inner stimulation. With his towel wrapped around his waist he poured an inch of bourbon from the hall mini-bar, and savored the liquid that slowly traveled down his throat.

He heard the chair creak, turned quickly, and nearly fell again, but Stella was there to wrap her arms around him, leaving the towel drop to the floor. The rest is history. Well, unwritten history, but memorable, none the less.

Luigi's came through once again. Later that same evening, putting all elevators behind him, Bob sat holding Stella's hand across the table, each one looking deeply into one another's eyes. The palms saved them from embarrassment when he leaned over and kissed her gently on the mouth. One would wonder if they would ever remember what was served for dinner that evening, not that it really matters.

El Chano had a totally different evening. Sydney was home from the hospital, but since she was still on antibiotics, she didn't feel she should drink the champagne that Chano offered.

"I don't think one sip will matter he urged. This is a celebration. You are home and looking exceptionally beautiful."

Flattery will get you nowhere. You know I am planning on returning to Israel, if they will have me. I left a message, and they should get back to me by tomorrow."

"This is today, my dear. And I plan on toasting one of the loveliest women I know, even though she shall soon fly out of my life."

Sydney had the grace to blush, but if truth be known, she was having a wonderful time, and even drank the champagne.

Now, never let it be said that El Chano was without charm. Sydney was in his arms before the champagne was gone. Dinner was ordered, and before the second kiss the doorbell rang, and a beautiful feast was soon laid before them, complete with more champagne. The evening was lovely, and even though the bedroom door stayed closed, hearts were opened and there would undoubtedly be a trip to Israel in Chano's future.

Now, never let it be said that the third man of this trio was left out. Luis still wore a sling, but his spirits were high. He called Margareta, the red head from the DA's office. No, there were no palms surrounding their table, but the embers from the fire cast a very inviting, rosy glow on her soft porcelain cheeks. A pink sparkling wine bubbled in their glasses, and one can be sure that their hearts were also abubble. (if that is possible.)

All in all, the evening was a delightful success for all the musketeers. Some might even say that it prepared them for what was to come. However, that would be much too clairvoyant for this mystery.

Bright and shiny faces gathered around the table at Mable's that Sunday morning. No one seemed to worry that the killer might decide to do his deed on a Sunday or even a Monday. No, this master criminal stuck to his playbook and seemed to enjoy the reaction of the audience.

Back at the mahogany desk, Bob looked around to see who would come up with the first idea. He waited.

Luis smiled. "How about this boss; why don't we have Connie, our police woman, who looks a lot like Sylvia, be our mock-victim of the night. We could do it one of two ways. First we could have one of the snakes bite her, and she dies a violent, slithering death on the floor. Or second, the one I like, is that she is found in the lavatory with her throat slit. I'll get the blood."

El Chano looked at Bob and winked. "The snake bite will be harder to pull off, but mimicking the lavatory murder would be easier. We just have to work out how the body is found. Oh, I see, much like before."

Luis smiled, "I kind of like that one, too. The only problem I have with it is, what if she is the killer?"

They all laughed. "Those are the risks in this business. We have to take chances, Luis," said Bob, "and my instinct tells me that she is the best candidate for the mock-victim. Good job, buddy. What do you think, Chano?"

Chano nodded. "I think we have a play. We'll work it up and get the props today, and then tomorrow is our dress rehearsal.:

"Then, Taco Tuesday," said Luis excitedly, is "opening night."

Chapter 24

The Final Act

"The spots look perfect," said El Chano as he joined the others at the mahogany desk. "They wouldn't tell me what paint they used for fear of upsetting the animal rights people," he laughed. "Anyway, the snakes are ready to go. I will pick them up tomorrow,

"What color are the spots?" asked Luis.

"Why orange, of course, almost red like the Black Widow. Poetic isn't it?"

"I don't know if that is exactly the term I would use," said Bob. Widows kill their mates; that's why they are called widows. Anyway, I guess in a macabre sort of way, it applies. Wish all killers could be identified by their spots."

El Chano laughed. "In a way they are, and when we catch this one, we will be spot on."

Each one threw the closest weapon they had at El Chano; mostly wadded up paper balls. He surrendered.

Bob had called Sylvia in for an interview to see if she would go along with their little charade, and as the boys were finishing their lunch sandwich, she was escorted to the mahogany desk. Another chair was drawn up and she sat expectantly, looking from one to another.

Bob took a deep breath, not relishing the job, at all. "I know this is an imposition, and you will probably also think we are out of our minds, but we are out to catch one of the most masterful killers we have ever encountered. We need your help."

Whatever Sylvia expected, this wasn't it. She all but preened herself as she nestled in her chair.

"Me? You really need my help?" She inched forward, and looked into Bob's deep blue eyes. "I want to see you catch this monster, too. Tell me what you want me to do?"

"It's a little theatrical," said El Chano. "We are going to put on a performance for the killer that we hope will trap him at his own game."

"You see," said Bob. "We are doing a re-enactment, and we are looking for someone who can be the victim. It is a really hard part, and actually, the star performance."

El Chano was giving Bob high marks for his psychology, especially as he watched Sylvia blush slightly, and then smile.

"What an enchanting idea. Of course, I will be happy to play the part. Just tell me what to wear. Oh, are there rehearsals?"

"Yes," Bob nodded. "Tomorrow night at 10:00."

"But, why so late?" asked Sylvia.

"This all has to be done in absolute secret," said Bob. We can't tell a soul. We don't want the killer to find out. That would kill the performance, if not more victims."

"Wow," thought Luis, "he actually said all that without a smile. And she bought the whole script. I guess we are putting on a play."

"Remember, Monday night. I will have an unmarked car pick you up about 9:45. This is high security. Top Secret."

El Chano shook his head after she left. "Well, do you think she can keep a secret?"

"Ha! Not normally, but I think she will do it this time for the sake of the performance, and for the biggest prize ever, the killer."

"Now, back to the preparations, said Bob. "El Chano, you have charge of the snakes. Luis, I will leave the blood to you. Remember we have to make it look as much like the last murder scene as possible. I will personally make sure that all the potential suspects are as far away from this place as possible during the rehearsal."

"What about the night of the murder, Taco Tuesday?"

"The invitations will be personally delivered and cars will be sent for each one. Yes, this, in part, is to make sure we have our suspects under observation. OK, fellow actors, go break a leg."

"I never understood that expression," said Luis. Seems barbaric to me."

"All right, all right. Good Luck. I'm starved."

At 10:00 Monday night the unmarked police cars started to arrive. The star, Sylvia, was the first to be escorted through the back door into the restaurant. They were setting up headquarters in the small conference room to the left of the kitchen, opposite side of the lavatories.

Stella had dutifully recorded her best scream the night before, and the blood was ready to be dribbled lavishly around the mock-victim and the lavatory floor. The helmet was hidden in Bob's trunk, and three of the gold nuggets were in his desk drawer, ready to be used to hold down the napkins on the tables used by the suspects. They were ready.

Sylvia was not happy with her position on the toilet, but after they coaxed her with celebrity status, placing her in the key position needed to catch a killer, she finally acquiesced. She decided to wear her black v-neck that would better show the blood and accentuate her endowments. Everyone was pleased with the play.

The only difficulty was with the employees. It took several lies from the DA's office that a new clue was uncovered, and needed to be investigated. No staff was to be allowed. On Taco Tuesday, most of the staff was also ordered to stay away. The police had a bartender and two policewomen who were happy to play their parts as waitresses. Two more plainclothes policemen were on duty behind the bar or on the floor as needed. Everyone agreed that the preparations were flawless; at least they hoped so.

Bob wondered if anyone actually slept that night. He stayed with Stella until almost midnight. Both of them were anxious. Stella was nervous about her scream.

"I wanted it to sound real, Bob, not made-up. You know, it's hard to scream for no reason at all."

"I should have come after you with a butcher knife," he teased. "Don't worry, you sounded great; like somebody was really trying to take a razor to your throat."

"I really want to be there, Bob. Isn't there some place I could hide?"

"I think I could arrange for you to take on your regular job as long as you stay in the background. Deal?"

"Deal!" she said, excitedly, followed by a yawn, and I have an extra uniform in the closet."

Bob kissed her goodnight, and made his way to his own condo. Suddenly his eyes were big and bright. He didn't believe in sleeping pills, and he knew that another beer wouldn't work either. Instead, he made his way to the kitchen and prepared a cup of cocoa, remembering what his mother always used to say. Something warm and soothing works better than something iced and intoxicating.

By the time he pulled back the blanket he was yawning. But that ended quickly when he let out a yelp! Something dark and menacing ran from under his pillow to the foot of the bed under the sheets.

He got on the phone and called his new best friend at the zoo. "Yes, it is still under there. What should I do? OK, I'll keep an eye out. He won't get by me. No, I will try not to kill it, but . . ."

By the time the zoo team arrived Bob was sitting in a chair facing the foot of the bed, holding a baseball bat. When the boys arrived they took over, positioned their nets, and with one fell swoop, threw back the covers and the net came down.

No one could tell who was more shocked, the tarantula or Bob. Well, actually, more thought the honors went to Bob.

"You must have some unusual friends," teased the one with the net, holding up the spider that measured about 3 ½ inches in diameter, not including it's fuzzy legs.

"He couldn't kill you, you know, even though he would have a good time trying. What kind of friends do you have, or do you think this was a scare tactic?"

"Yep, it was meant to scare me. I work at homicide and we are about to catch one of the deadliest killers in years. Just trying to rattle me.:

"Ha! Did it work?"

'I'm not sleeping in my bed, if that is what you mean. I am going to strip the damn thing and throw it all in the wash. After that I may spray the bed with insecticide."

They all laughed, and took the furry creature back to the zoo. "Don't worry, we'll find out how he got out."

Bob made his way back to Stella's and asked if he could spend the night on her couch.

"Why the couch?" she questioned.

"Because I have to sleep!" he boldly replied.

The sun peeked through the drapes and signaled another "Taco Tuesday." Bob tried to roll over to block out the sun but instantly fell on the floor and found himself wound up in the blanket, signaling a very restless night.

He smelled the coffee followed by the delightful aroma of bacon. "Do I have time for a 10 minute shower? he asked. I won't take long. She nodded and he took two sips of coffee and ran to his condo. He entered cautiously, wondering if he had any more nocturnal visitors.

"Until a person experiences it himself, he will never understand how unnerving it really is."

He checked the shower for more zoo creatures, then turned it on while he laid out his wardrobe for the day. It took him 15 minutes before he put his fork into the eggs accompanied with a bite of bacon.

"Yes, this is definitely an improvement over my former lifestyle," he whispered to himself.

The dark mahogany desk stood waiting for the three musketeers. The jelly donuts were in the box, two apiece, this time. The blood was carefully camouflaged at the back of the desk. The coffee cups soon arrived, each being carried by their owner.

El Chano took his usual wooden seat, as did Luis. Bob had the permanent, soft cushioned desk chair; after all it was his desk.

They all sat quietly for a minute, sipping their coffee and taking a bite of the donut, trying not to let the jelly ooze out the back.

Yes, it was Taco Tuesday, and there were nine hours to go before curtain time. They could all feel the lag and each one in his own way wondered if he could last that long.

"It's the waiting that is so difficult," said El Chano. "I much prefer action. No, not the kind you had last night mi amigo, with that bug in your bed."

"That was no bug, but I knew you guys would have to experience it to understand. Anyway, it is over and the condo is being searched and exterminated by experts today."

"Sorry to laugh, boss, but just listening to the story is rather funny, and no, I would not like the experience. I just can't figure out why he went to all that trouble."

"Drama," said Bob. "This guy is an actor at heart, and now he is staring in his very own production."

"What is nagging at me," said El Chano, "is the script he may be writing for tonight. Gentlemen, if he is planning another murder, I don't see how we can prevent it."

"We have to preempt," said Bob. "That's the whole point of our production. We want to beat him to the punch. We want our performance to not only rattle him, but prevent another murder."

"I can't think about it any more, boss. I keep looking for flaws and I am afraid I will find one. If you guys don't mind, and if you don't need me for a while, I'll go down to the gym and work out. That seems to help."

El Chano nodded, "Luis, that's the best plan I have heard all day. Come on, let's sweat."

Bob shook his head, and instead, just leaned back in his chair and closed his eyes. The spider episode finally left his thinking and he was back.

"Darn clever of that guy to try to rattle me. This tells me that he has something planned for tonight. That's the rub. Whatever it is it could throw our whole performance into disarray. Good God, what else can we do. We just have to go ahead with our plans and tell all the boys to keep watch. It has to work. When you are up against a mastermind you never know what will happen."

Bob stopped short. "Wait a minute," he chastised himself. "We have been calling this guy a mastermind and we've convinced ourselves. Hell, he is just a killer that has gotten away with it for who knows how long. OK, this is his Waterloo. Yes sir, Captain Nelson, he'll be ready to string up."

"Exactly eight hours later, the players were assembled in the conference room, and went over their duties once more. Bob saw to the props, and placed the motorcycle helmet on the table that held the menus, all in plain sight of whoever entered the restaurant.

The black and gold nuggets were strategically anchoring the napkins on the tables. The speaker was also secured on the stage and ready to broadcast the scream.

Exactly at 6:00 the police cars drove up with the guests for the evening. The smaller tables were used instead of the celebrity table so the snakes would be more visible.

If there had been a curtain, it would have opened, the orchestra would have paused, and the play would then begin.

El Chano's brother Antonio, and his sister Rosa arrived along with Sylvia who all were escorted to a table for four with the place cards indicating the seating. The next group arrived with El Chano leading the group that included Don Diego and Manuel. The chairs for Gladys and Juan were removed leaving only their place cards to remind everyone of their fate.

El Chano chose not to sit at the table, but to remove his card so as to accentuate Clare's absence. Bob stepped forward.

Ladies and gentlemen; I want to thank you for your attendances this evening. Our department has been working diligently to bring an end to this investigation. We are almost there."

There were ooos and aahs. So far no one paid any undo attention to the gold nuggets on the table even though Bob knew they were recognized by at least one of the guests. He also watched closely as they all entered to see the expression when they each saw the helmet. Yes, someone did flinch, but for now, only El Chano knows who it was.

We must remember that the killer has been acting for quite some time, bamboozling the police, so it was not surprising that no one paid undue attention to the gold.

The waiters began serving the margaritas, and miniature tacos were placed on each table. The atmosphere lightened, but everyone kept looking from side to side to see what might happen next. There was an aura of expectancy, a sense of something unknown that was about to enter their lives that actually made the skin crawl.

Antonio was drinking too fast, and by the time the third margarita arrived he was fidgety. Most of the others were sipping on their second drink, and gobbling down the horsdoeuvres. Antonio started fumbling the nugget and holding it up to the table candle.

"Hey," he stuttered, "this looks like something I saw in a museum once. Wow, brother, is this real gold or fool's gold?"

Everyone started looking more closely at the rock in front of them. Manuel picked it up and turned to Bob who was standing close by.

"What the hell is going on here? I have seen these before. What kind of a joke are you trying to pull?"

Manuel became more agitated. "My daughter is gone because of rocks like these. The mother load; ha! What is worth losing your only child? You even have her place card with the empty chair to torment me. She is not coming back. Once they are gone they are gone."

Manuel rose, more agitated now, wondering who he could vent his anger on. "And you!" He turned to Don Diego. "You did this, you corrupted her. She thought she loved you, but you used that love to do your bidding. You taught her greed. You taught her to kill."

The SCREAM vibrated around the room, louder than ever. Everyone froze. Everyone that is except Don Diego, who jumped up, visibly shaken.

"Who is that?" he yelled, his voice cracked and garbled. "She's dead, she's dead," and he dashed from the room with Bob and El Chano on his heels.

Manuel started to follow, but two waiters blocked him. He, too, was noticeably unhinged.

When they reached the lavatories, Don Diego dashed to the stall and pulled it open. There she was. The blood was still dripping onto the floor and running close to his foot. He jumped. He screamed again, pointed to the ring on her finger, and ran back to the dining room, looking for a way to escape.

He was escorted back to his seat at the same moment that three snakes started dashing around the floor, not knowing which way to go.

To say there was mass confusion would be an understatement. No one knew whether to jump on their chair or run from the room. When Don Diego saw the snakes, he did jump on his chair and pointed.

"The spot, the spot, these are venomous. They kill. Run for your lives."

Everyone watched Bob and El Chano to see what they would do. At that moment two reptile keepers scooped up the snakes with their nets. One of them was wearing the motorcycle helmet. It was a lot like a horror film. The unexpected kept coming.

This time both Manuel and Don Diego screamed together. The sound of men screaming is somehow more terrifying. Probably because it is, again, the unexpected.

"You killed her, you killed her," croaked Manuel, and this time he drew a gun from his stocking.

Now everyone became alarmed. There was no question that he intended to kill.

"He is a madman, a madman," yelled Don Diego. "Somebody stop him. I don't want to die. Yes, I killed Clare; Juan, too, but they deserved to die. They would have interfered with my plans. Clare wanted half of everything. She had to die."

Manuel raised the gun higher, but El Chano grabbed his arm, and the gun went off with the barrel pointing to the ceiling.

Don Diego covered his face and began to cry. Two officers, one with cuffs, took him from the room. It was utterly quiet.

Manuel slumped in his chair, perspiration running down his face. El Chano faced him. "OK Manuel, you, too, killed a man. Was it Pete Stebens, the one we dug up from the floor of the mine?"

"He was my partner. We found the mine together. We had been friends for years, but gold does something to a man. He wanted it all. It's gold fever. Greed, greed."

"But you killed. And I think that was from greed too.:"

"It was the mother lode. Don't you understand. The mother lode. And now, Gladys is gone. It doesn't really matter any more."

"Why didn't you register your claim, or try to buy the land as well?"

"Can you imagine what would happen? Thousands would come. It would become nother gold rush. We would lose in the end, you know. Probably would have been killed. You have no idea what gold fever does to a man."

"I am beginning to understand," grimaced El Chano. He rose from the chair and walked over to Bob. "Well, are we done here, amigo?"

Bob nodded, "Yes, we are done, but I am not feeling the usual triumph from closing a murder case. Kind of bitter-sweet."

Bob turned to the rest of the party, "We are closing up shop now, folks. We will serve one more drink to toast the end of this production, and the end to the Taco Tuesday Murders."

When Bob and El Chano were left sipping their brew, a sleepy Stella sat down with them. "It's over Bob, let's find an island someplace. You deserve it."

"Wait a minute," said Bob, "there is a more important issue at hand, remember?"

Stella thought for a minute and smiled. "Bob, not here in front of El Chano!"

"Why not, my dear. I need to know. Will you marry me?"

Before she could speak, he reached in his pocket and pulled out a small box, opened the lid, took out the sapphire and diamond ring, and waited for that one word."

"Yes!"

The ring was placed on her finger.

Chapter 25

Never Say Goodbye

The next morning Bob sat at the mahogany desk with coffee cup in hand. There were no jelly donuts. Nobody seemed to be in the mood. Even Luis, who sat with his elbow on the end of the desk, his head drooped in his hand, had nothing to say.

Then all of a sudden, a brown paper bag plopped on the desk.

"Look at you two," commented El Chano. "Two of the saddest sacks I have ever seen; and no wonder, you didn't have your sugar."

Bob jumped up and clasped his shoulders. "Mi amigo, you are just what we needed. This was a hell of a case. We couldn't have done it without you. I wanted to thank you properly. How about dinner tonight at Luigi's?"

"That works for me, but I have other news. This experience with you, Bob, has given my life a new perspective. My construction business is in good hands, and I am now free to pursue other avenues. What do you think of the idea of me opening a detective agency?"

Both Bob and Luis clapped at once and let out a yahoo!

"That's all I needed," said Chano. "You two are my greatest supporters. I haven't decided just where as yet, but we can talk over dinner tonight. Now Bob, don't you have a date to share with me?"

"Date? Oh, yes. Two months on the 15th. Will you be my best man?"

"I wouldn't miss it for the world if you will do me the favor if that day should ever come for me."

"The hell with the donuts," said Luis. "We need something to toast the upcoming nuptial as well as the upcoming El Chano Detective Agency. I need a brew."

"Luis, it's only 11:00," said Bob.

"You know the saying: It's five o'clock somewhere. Come on," urged El Chano.

And they came.

The End.